RIVE
of
SECRETS

GRISELDA GIFFORD

RIVER
of
SECRETS

Andersen Press • London

First published in 2002 by
Andersen Press Limited,
20 Vauxhall Bridge Road, London SW1V 2SA

British Library Cataloguing in Publication Data available
ISBN 1 84270 045 6

Typeset by FiSH Books, London WC1
Printed and bound in Great Britain by the Guernsey Press Company Ltd.,
Guernsey, Channel Islands

*To Jim and all the family
and in loving memory of another granny,
Jill Denton*

Chapter 1

It was all over now. Mum was married to boring old Matthew Turner, and we'd moved here, to Gran's old home, Folly Farm. *And* I was landed with Matthew's unfriendly son Jez. I wished I could run away as I looked out of the window of my dear gran's old room and tried not to cry. I was glad that mist hid the river where she had drowned so mysteriously a few months ago. Suddenly I knew what I had to do – I had to find out what really happened. Supposing she'd been murdered? 'I'll find out, Gran,' I said and I hoped she'd hear me from wherever she was.

I wished I could talk to Mum about Gran's death but she was light years away, enclosed in a space capsule called Love. For her sake, I made an effort to talk to Jez at the wedding but I might as well not have bothered. Obviously he didn't like me, so why should I go on trying?

At any moment, I felt I'd turn round and see Gran smiling. 'Let's do something daft, Fran,' she'd say, and we'd tear off to swim in the river early in the morning. She'd always loved swimming and although she was well over sixty she still boasted about her weekly half mile in the local pool. Sometimes we'd go off in the old rowing boat for a picnic, or sometimes she had a

1

gardening fit on and I'd help her dig the vegetable plot. Well, at least I'd be sleeping in her old room where a sort of essence of Gran lingered.

Wasn't that someone – waving at me through the leaves of the apple tree? Then I looked again and there was nothing.

'I think we'll give Jez this room,' Mum said behind me.

I whirled round, furious. 'But it's mine – I mean, it was Gran's – why should *he* have it?' I could hardly speak.

'Don't get so worked up, Fran. He needs room for his computer and the other bedroom's smaller – but you'll still have the view. After all, that's where you slept before. We want to make Jez feel welcome, Fran darling. Try to put yourself in his shoes.'

Why didn't she try to put herself in mine?

There wasn't much time to think after that. Matthew and Jez arrived, then the two lots of removal men. They did a complicated dance, avoiding each other. When they'd gone, we started unpacking the endless cardboard boxes. There was far too much of everything, even though some of Gran's furniture had been sold.

A mournful baying started up outside and our dog Sophie joined in from her temporary prison in the old stable. 'That's Bas,' said Jez. I followed him outside. A mega-sad face was peering out of the Turners' car window, his deep-set eyes set in a welter of worried furrows.

I couldn't help laughing. 'You didn't say you had a bloodhound!'

'Don't be stupid.' Jez's voice cracked on a high note. 'We told you Bas was a basset-hound.' Really, that boy has nil sense of humour. He stroked the dog's high forehead. 'I can't see why he had to stay in the car,' he complained.

Later on, when Jez and I were upstairs organising our rooms, the doorbell went. Mum called out in a muffled voice from the linen cupboard. 'Be an angel and answer it, Fran. Matthew's gone to the shops.'

I recognised Mrs Gooding from the funeral. She was weighed down by Gran's huge black cat, Obediah. A small boy and a girl who might be about my age were staring at me as if I'd come from another planet. I was wearing my chopped-off jeans, which were more fray than cloth, a shrunken tee-shirt and my favourite big black Oxfam hat to cheer me up.

'We've mostly fed him in your garden because he's got the cat-flap but he follows Fay over to us. My husband's not very keen on cats.' Mrs Gooding smiled nervously. She put a hand to her face but not before I'd seen a dark bruise just below her eye.

Mum joined me at the door and took the sagging bundle in her arms, smiling and thanking Mrs Gooding. 'I didn't realise about your husband. It was so kind of you to offer to feed Obediah.' I could see her trying not to look at the bruise.

The children went on staring so I stared back – I'd been too upset at the funeral to notice them but Gran told us on the telephone before she died about the Gooding children and that the family had recently moved to one of the new houses next to Folly Farm. She'd sounded specially fond of the little boy. 'They're an unhappy family,' she'd said, mysteriously. 'I'm very worried about them.'

'This is Robin,' Mrs Gooding said. 'My baby.' He went on sucking his thumb as if he agreed. 'And Fay.' She looked like Alice in Wonderland, with her old-fashioned, flowered dress, long fair hair and a blue hair-band.

'Hi,' I said.

Mum told me always to look people in the eyes but Fay didn't. She mumbled something and stared at the holes in my jeans. Perhaps in her Enid Blyton world she'd not met much grunge.

'Where's Granny Lee?' Robin asked plaintively.

Mrs Gooding said, 'He was ever so fond of your mother, Mrs Turner. Always called her Granny Lee.' She looked as if she might cry. 'It was all such a shock. She was so kind to us.' Her voice tailed off.

There was a deep rumble from Bas. Obediah wriggled, leaped out of Mum's arms and ran off. 'I'd ask you in, Mrs Gooding,' Mum said, 'but we're in such a mess. Maybe Fay would like to come round some time. Fran and my stepson, Jeremy, don't know any children round here.'

'My husband's away.' Mrs Gooding paused. 'Perhaps they could come and have tea with us tomorrow? I'll make some of my fairy cakes.'

'I'm sure they'd love to,' Mum said although I nudged her with my elbow and Mrs Gooding smiled and hurried her children away before I could refuse.

Jez was braver than me and refused to come but Mum said it wouldn't hurt me to get to know Fay. 'She looks weird!' I wailed but Mum was opening another cardboard box and didn't answer.

At first, Bas did not like our dog, Sophie. When she bounced up to him he growled and ran at her on his short, bandy legs, even though she was much bigger than he was. I shouted at Bas and Jez scowled at me and led him away.

I patted poor Sophie and walked down the lawn. A small green apple bounced off my shoulder as we went under the tree. I thought I heard someone call my name so I looked up. The leaves fluttered, as they had before although it was a totally windless summer morning but I couldn't see beyond the thick lower leaves and small apples.

I called Sophie, who was sniffing and barking by the barn door, which Gran kept locked. There were probably rats amongst the junk.

We wandered down the garden to the river and, like a true water dog, she jumped in, swimming towards the ducks on the opposite bank. 'Sophie!' I yelled but she took no notice, and scrambled up as the ducks flew off with a wild quacking. The cows in the field beyond trotted towards the stupid dog who seemed to have gone deaf. She'd be in trouble with the farmer!

I could swim across but it meant undressing. Then I saw Gran's old rowing boat, tied to a ring on the wooden landing-stage. After what had happened to her, I didn't want to go in it ever again but I had to get Sophie.

I undid the rope and rowed hard to the other side. The River Dene is quite wide here and by the time I reached Sophie, the bullocks were standing, heads lowered, ready to charge her.

I held on to an overhanging branch and shouted at her. She pretended to be deaf and barked at the cattle. I tied up to a tree root, jumped into thick mud, scrabbled up the bank and waved the bullocks off, hanging on to Sophie's collar. Tugging her back I stopped with a jolt. The boat had somehow got loose and it was being pushed this way and that by the current, going downstream!

I stumbled along the river bank, slipping on cow dung and stinging my ankles on the thick nettles. With luck, the boat might drift against the big bend in the river, near the churchyard, as it had when Gran – no, I couldn't think of that now. Sweat was trickling between my shoulder-blades and flies swarmed round my head. I swore out loud. Somehow I got Sophie under strands of barbed wire but I heard my jeans tear.

Now I could see the river again. The boat had been caught against the opposite bank. A girl was waving at me from the churchyard wall. 'Catch the rope!' I yelled. She scrambled down and grabbed the boat's prow, just as it was drifting off the bank again. To my surprise, she jumped in and swiftly rowed across the river to me, throwing me the rope with a quick, expert twist of her hand.

'Thanks!' I said, getting in with Sophie, who nearly turned the boat over as she rushed to lick the girl's face. She wasn't usually so friendly with strangers.

'Not much good at knots, are you?' She rowed us back to the graveyard side and I clung on to a tuft of grass while she leaped out. Though she seemed strong she was smaller than me. There was mud on her shorts and her shirt-sleeve was torn. I wanted to talk to her but she just said, 'See you around!' and climbed over the wall into the churchyard.

It was hard work, rowing back against the current. As I rounded the bend in the river I saw Mum, Matthew and Bas waiting for me. They all looked angry.

'Why did you go off like that?' Mum shouted as soon as she saw me. 'And in the boat, of all things.' She was dead white and almost in tears.

'You upset your mum,' Matthew said quietly. 'Specially after your gran...' He stopped and tied the boat to the big metal ring.

'I was trying to catch Sophie,' I said angrily. 'But I'm sorry, Mum.' I wasn't going to apologise to *him*.

Later on, Mum asked me to help get supper. 'What about Jez? He's been in his room for hours.' And I'd been dead bored, putting kitchen stuff away.

She turned to me, her face flushed from the oven. 'Matthew told him to get his things straight. I do hope you're going to be nice to him, Fran. Apparently he went right into his shell after his mother died two years ago in that climbing accident. He won't even talk about it.' She looked at me. 'Try to get through to him, Fran.'

I shivered. How would I feel if that had happened to Mum? 'Poor Jez – but I suppose he's had a bit more time to get used to his mum's death.' I knew I was being selfish but something sore and angry inside me drove me on. 'Nobody cares how *I'm* feeling. It's so weird, being here without Gran. I loved staying with her while you were working.'

'I know,' Mum said quietly. 'After all, Fran, she was my mother, you know.'

She looked so sad that I hugged her. 'I'm sorry, Mum. But you seem so happy with Matthew – as if nothing had happened.'

'Gran wouldn't have wanted me to be miserable all the time,' Mum said. 'And it would be hard on Matthew.' She smiled. As if on cue, we could hear his voice upstairs, talking to Jez. Perhaps he was telling him to come and help.

'Mum . . . ' I hesitated. 'You didn't tell me much about the inquest and you were so upset at the time I didn't like to ask. What does an Open Verdict mean?'

'Just that.' Mum put the lettuce in a tea towel and shook it savagely. 'They don't know exactly what happened. The postmortem – that's when a doctor looks at the body (I felt rather sick when she said this) – showed only that she'd had a heart attack, probably from

8

the shock of the cold water but nobody knows why she was out in the boat in her nightie in the early morning and why she fell out of it.' She stopped and thumped down plates and cutlery on the scrubbed wooden table I had known so long. 'Old people do strange things. Maybe she'd taken sleeping pills or something and they made her dizzy.'

She fetched celery from one of the cardboard boxes still on the floor. 'A good thing I thought of bringing food with us. I don't think the village shop stocks much.' She was changing the conversation, just as she had ever since the accident.

I wanted to shake her. 'I think she was murdered!' I said but Matthew and Jez came in then and I don't think Mum heard. Nobody else was going to bother about an old woman's death. It was up to me.

Jez wheezed a bit at supper. 'Asthma,' Matthew explained as Jez went out. I felt sorry for him so I went upstairs with a mug of tea and hesitated outside Gran's room, as I still thought of it. When I went in, I did wish time could go backwards and she would be there.

Jez was staring at his computer screen. 'Are you okay now?' I asked.

He grunted and didn't bother to look round as I put the mug down. I glanced at the screen and saw he was typing something. He changed the screen at that moment with the mouse and it was empty, except for the pulsing cursor.

Well, for Mum's sake I'd try. 'Sorry about your

asthma.' He just grunted again. His thin shoulders were tense and he sat very still. 'And you must miss your mum,' I crashed on. 'I know what it's like, because of my gran dying. I was totally gutted at the time and I still miss her, a lot.'

At last he turned round. 'Yes – that was an awful shock for you. But she was old, after all. My mother was only thirty-five.'

Well, of course I left him to it then. If he hadn't said that, about Gran, I might never have gone to the Goodings the next day but I was so mad at him I just wanted to get away. I took Sophie outside.

The garden glowed in the setting sun and there wasn't a breath of wind but, as I walked under the apple tree, the leaves moved again and another apple fell at my feet. This one was almost ripe. I picked it up and noticed that there was a bite out of it. I guessed it must be the squirrels.

I found myself thinking about that girl who'd caught the boat. There was something I liked about her. I hoped I'd see her again.

Chapter 2

I woke up early that first morning. Half asleep, I looked round the familiar room and felt happy. What would we do today? We... then I remembered. Gran was dead and I was trapped here, with the alien Turners. I had to get away from the house, to find out more about Gran's death.

Almost before I'd swallowed my muesli, Jez and I were swept into more unpacking. After boring ages at it, I said I'd see what Sophie was up to in the garden and Jez followed me, carrying a couple of empty boxes, Bas behind him. He looked at Sophie, who was trotting up and down the riverbank, grumbling gently to herself as if she wanted to plunge in and get to the bullocks again. 'What sort of dog is she?'

'She's half labrador, half poodle,' I explained. 'A poodledor.'

'A labradoodle sounds better.' He actually smiled so I grinned back. Maybe we'd get on, after all. Bas was wagging his tail now and we watched while he trotted to see Sophie. She turned and they sniffed at each other, carefully. Bas sat down, looking serious, while Sophie wagged her tail. 'I think they'll get on now,' Jez said and I agreed.

After a sandwich lunch, Matthew got Jez to help him move furniture that had just been dumped by the removal men in the middle of each room. This would be my chance to get away. Mum had been complaining she was short of cleaning materials so I offered to go to the village shop with Sophie. I'd have taken Bas too, only he was following Jez about. I suppose the poor dog felt strange and insecure in a new house.

Gran and I had often taken the short cut through the woods and I felt sort of sad-happy to be there again, walking on a carpet of last year's leaves under the beech trees.

Sophie ran ahead, barking. When I caught up she was wagging her tail at the girl I'd met yesterday, who was holding a rope tied to a branch above a steep bank. She kicked off, with a scream of laughter, as she was swung down towards the river. One of her wellies fell off, and then she swung back so fast I had to jump out of the way. Down she went again, leaping off the rope near the bottom, landing deep in a patch of bracken. Sophie slithered after her, barking and wagging her tail, leaping on the girl and licking her face.

'Want a go?' she asked, picking up her boot.

I couldn't remember the rope being there before, when I'd come this way with Gran. The branch didn't look very strong. 'I'm heavier than you,' I said.

'You're scared! Cowardy-cowardy custard! I dare you!' she shouted.

'I'm not scared! Chuck me the rope.'

I pushed off the scuffed earth. I skimmed over bushes, bracken, saw a glint of the river far below, then I was swinging back again, bumping the bank. As the rope took me down again she shouted: 'Jump!'

I jumped and landed in something prickly. She laughed as I disentangled myself from straggling brambles. I was glad I was wearing jeans.

'I'd like to parachute jump,' she said. 'Just think of swinging above the earth.' I wasn't going to admit the idea didn't grab me. She grinned at me. 'Let's go to my secret den. I've got jam sandwiches for my dinner.'

I was still hungry and it was tempting. Then I thought of the shopping and tea with the Goodings. 'Sorry – maybe tomorrow?' I said. 'I'm Fran – we've just come to live here.'

'I'm Denny.' She was busy replaiting her long hair. 'My family's lived round here for ever.'

'See you tomorrow?' I asked her. 'I've got this boring stepbrother and stepfather and I'd like to get away.'

'Perhaps they won't be so bad when you get used to them,' Denny said. 'They've got to get to know you. The boy looks a bit sad to me.'

'When did you see him?'

She grinned. 'I've been up the apple tree and on your barn roof. I've been coming there when the house was empty, too.'

So I hadn't imagined the leaves moving – somehow she'd managed to hide herself. I took a deep breath but my voice wobbled as I said, 'Did you see my gran?

Before...before she drowned in the river a few months ago? I want to find out just what happened.'

'Yes, I heard about it and I'm sorry...It must be dreadful for you.' She hesitated. 'But I can't help you. Maybe that lonely girl next door might know something. See you tomorrow.' She ran back up the path.

I came out of the woods into the village opposite the square-towered church. The last time I'd been there was at Gran's funeral when I'd stared at her small coffin in the aisle and felt a great emptiness.

I tied Sophie's lead to the ice-cream sign outside the village shop. I was piling things into my wire basket when I heard a familiar voice outside talking to Sophie. 'Poor old girl! Won't they let you in, then?' It was Hills, Hillary Hardy, Gran's old friend from way back. I think they'd even been to school together.

'Hullo there!' she boomed at me when she came inside. Her large hip brushed a Special Offer pyramid of Doggomeat tins and knocked them down. I helped her pick them up and collected six of them for my basket. 'I heard on the grapevine you were coming to Folly Farm. Just what Frances would have wanted.' I was named Frances after Gran.

This wasn't the moment to ask her about Gran's last days. When I paid, Mrs King, the shopkeeper, said she was sorry about Gran. 'Such a nice lady.' Stupidly, my eyes started leaking out tears. Then I pulled myself together. If I was going to do detective work, I could start here.

'Did you see my gran the week before it happened?' I asked Mrs King.

'She came in the day before and looking ever so well, too. I remember it because she said she was going to make some cakes for the children next door. Quite taken up with the little boy, she was. And of course with poor Mrs Gooding's problems – that husband of hers! He was shouting at his daughter here, in the shop. No knowing what he does at home.' Mrs King sniffed disapprovingly.

Hills offered to drive me home. It was a good chance to ask her about Gran so I hopped in. Sophie whined nervously as we took off with a crashing of gears.

'When did you last see Gran alive?' I asked bravely.

'Just the day before, dear.' Hills' voice quivered a little. 'The day she died we were going on the Silver Threads outing – in the Crumbly Coach, as she called it.' She tooted at an alarmed cyclist who swerved and nearly fell off. 'Mind you – she did have one worry. Damn!' The road was blocked by a horse-box and she braked just in time, so hard that Sophie was jolted forward, thrusting her nose between the seats.

'What was it?' I asked, calming Sophie.

'Those children next door and their poor mother, living with that awful husband. She said she might report him.'

'What for?'

'She suspected cruelty. You mustn't worry about it, Fran. You see, it's difficult to prove. But I think your gran had spoken to Mr Gooding and he'd shouted at her,

saying she should mind her own business or else...'
Hills squeezed her car past the horse-box, forcing it into
the side and the driver made a rude sign at her.

'Or else what?' I asked

'Just a threat, nothing more.' Hills crashed the gears
again and then said: 'I wondered if someone broke in to
the farm and somehow she tried to get away in the boat.
But the police didn't find any signs of a break-in.'

'Everyone else thinks it was an accident,' I said. 'Did
she take sleeping pills? They could've made her woozy.'

Hills smiled. 'Definitely no! She'd hardly take an
aspirin. Yes, it must have been some kind of accident
though why your gran would go out in her night things
in the boat beats me. She wasn't going ga-ga, you
know.' She braked violently outside Folly Farm. 'But
there's nothing we can do now. Come and see me soon,
Fran. I dug out some old snaps to show you of your gran
and me. They might amuse you.'

I thanked her and she drove away with a terrible clash
of gears.

I'd always liked Hills and maybe she could help me
work out how Gran died. I was even more sure now it
wasn't an accident. Supposing that Mr Gooding had
attacked her? But wouldn't it have shown at the postmortem, if he'd hit her? Maybe he'd given her such a
fright that she had a heart attack. Then, scared, he'd
bundled her into the boat and somehow she'd fallen
out. I sighed. It was hard doing detective work and
horrible to think that my darling gran had been bullied

or scared. Somehow I'd work on Fay and get to the truth.

Everyone was too busy to thank me for the shopping but Mum said she was glad I'd seen Hills. 'She thought the world of your gran,' she added sadly.

Jez and Matthew were putting anything we couldn't squeeze into the house in the loft and Mum kept me busy helping her put a zillion books in the shelves – mostly Matthew's, of course, so I was glad to escape to the Goodings at tea-time.

Fay answered the door. This time she looked a real freak in a too-long white pleated skirt and a lacy pink long-sleeved jumper embroidered with bobbly roses. 'Come in – you're late!' she snapped. I wondered why I'd come.

The hall carpet was pale pink and had a plastic runner down the centre. I followed Fay to the living room. Mrs Gooding was staring into the garden with a strange, glazed look. I suppose she was quite pretty for her age but her face was dead white and the bruise still showed. Robin sat on her lap, sucking his thumb and holding something. He had a sticking-plaster on his arm.

Mrs Gooding smiled vaguely at me and we sat down to tea, tiny sandwiches and dainty little cakes that went in one bite. Robin dropped one of his sandwiches and immediately Mrs Gooding leaped up and fetched a cloth. 'Oh dear, Daddy won't like a mark on the new carpet, will he?' she said and Robin immediately burst into tears. 'My husband likes things just so, Frances,' she explained. Her hands were shaking. When she sat down again she swallowed a tablet with a sip of tea.

'I hate Dad!' Fay burst out so loudly that I jumped.

Mrs Gooding frowned at her. 'You mustn't say things like that. Your father's under a lot of strain at the moment. He's a sales representative and travels a lot, Frances.' She looked apprehensively at the door, as if he might walk in at any moment. 'Take Frances to your room, Fay.' She shut her eyes.

'What's your dad like?' I asked when we were going upstairs.

'I hate him!' she said again. 'He's a bully.'

I thought of Mrs Gooding's bruise. 'Does he hit you?'

We were on the landing now and she grabbed my arm. 'Sometimes. But you mustn't tell anyone, Mum says or They might split the family up.'

I wondered who They were but there was no chance to ask because she was going into her bedroom. I stood there, gobsmacked.

Dolls – I was surrounded by their blank, staring faces ranged on shelves all round the room. There were baby dolls, Spanish dolls, Japanese dolls, old-fashioned dolls in long dresses... Eyes, on me... 'How many?' I asked feebly.

'Oh – forty-two, I think,' she said. She flung open her window and stared out. 'Sometimes I think about making a huge bonfire of them. *She* thinks I like them. Well, I suppose I did, when I was little but I'm twelve now. Nobody has dolls at my age. Some of them are hers, only Dad won't have them in their room.' She stared out. 'I thought I saw someone swimming in the river,' she said in a strange voice.

I looked over her shoulder, at the shimmer of the river flowing beyond the fence at the end of the garden. 'Nobody there.'

I'd never seen such a tidy room. 'Where's all your things?' I asked, thinking of my own comfortable clutter that Mum said was a tip.

'In the cupboard. If I get untidy, Dad locks me in till I've cleared up.' I gawped at her, my mind boggling. 'I'm glad your stepbrother didn't come,' she went on. 'I don't like boys.'

'Jez would be okay if he didn't act like he thinks I'm just a child,' I said. 'I'm sort of sorry for him because his mother is dead but he doesn't think my gran dying matters half as much. And it does! I think she was *murdered*.'

I watched Fay carefully. She went as white as her skirt. 'Why... why do you think that?' she stammered. 'I heard the police didn't find anything.'

'I just think someone else was involved. Gran was so sensible. She'd never have gone out in her boat dressed like that! I'm going to find out how she died!' I said loudly.

Fay clutched at my arm. 'No! There's nothing to find out. You'll just get more upset.' She saw me staring and let go my arm. 'Your gran was kind – even if she did like Robin more than me.' She swallowed. 'Promise not to tell and I'll show you my special place.' She carefully unfolded a scarf from an immaculate drawer.

I was curious. 'Okay.'

I followed her outside into the green shade of a willow tree which grew against the back of our barn, bounding the two gardens. She waved the scarf at me. 'You've got to wear this and swear not to tell anyone about my magic.'

'I swear – okay,' I said, to get it over with as quickly as possible. It seemed a bit babyish, going blindfold when I could see where we were going.

'Robin didn't like the scarf over his eyes,' Fay muttered as she guided me along. 'That's why he screamed. I wasn't hurting him like she thought.' What was she on about? I stumbled along and then she told me to crawl, so I took the scarf off. We were under the willow tree, and Fay's feet were disappearing through a hole she'd made in a boarded-up door.

'Why'd you take the scarf off?' she asked angrily when we were both inside.

'It's a silly kids' game,' I said scornfully. The light from the opening showed me that we were, as I thought, in Gran's barn. All the garden stuff and junk was huddled at the far side. This end was almost empty and Fay darted off lighting candles, stuck into jam-jars. She held one in her hand, like a torch and it threw strange shadows on the pictures she'd stuck to the rough walls. There was a huge man in a black suit with an angry expression, waving a stick at a cringing stick-girl. Fay turned and saw me looking. 'That's a dream I get.' The man was obviously her dad: a pretty obvious dream.

In the next picture, a figure dressed in a long green dress stood protectively in front of the stick-girl. Rays shot from the green woman's hands and were obviously shrinking the angry man to doll-size. There was something definitely creepy about the pictures.

Fay lit the last two candles on either side of a weird lump of wood on a box. The candlelight made it seem to have holes for eyes and a sticking-out bit like a nose. She'd stuck on bendy twigs to look like hair. Below it stood a jug filled with leaves and red berries. 'Rowan – for protection,' Fay murmured, fingering a piece of wood that hung around her neck.

I nearly giggled when she lifted her hands in the air and brought them down slowly so she was crouching in front of the bit of wood. 'Worship the Green Woman!' she said in a funny churchy voice. She got up and looked at me. 'I found her on the beach on our last holiday. Dad had done a lot of shouting and Mum kept wanting to go home. I suppose you'd call it driftwood but I know I was meant to have it. The Green Man's magic is rubbish compared to the Green Woman's.' She looked at me. 'You don't believe she's got powers, do you? But she has. Last week she made a spell to send my dad away and he did, for his job as a sales rep. The Green Woman won't do bad things. And she's for the rivers, the trees, green places – she hates people who hurt animals or cut down trees.'

'Get her to find out how my gran died.' If I kept on at Fay, she might crack and give her dad away.

There was a loud thud on the roof and a slithering sound, then the clunk of a slate falling off. I looked up. Were those eyes staring at me through the hole?

Fay screamed and clutched at me.

Chapter 3

'It's a ghost!' she whispered. There was a thud as she dropped the candle she was holding and it landed on a pile of drawing paper which immediately caught fire.

'You total geek!' I shouted, throwing a mouldy old sack on top of the flames, putting them out.

Fay clung to me and I tried to shake her off. Then I heard her mum calling.

At once she let go, blew out the altar candles and led the way out, through a small door in the barn. I noticed a broken slate at my feet and I quickly looked up at the barn roof but the 'ghost' had gone. Had Denny been up there?

Fay looked through the willow leaves. 'My mum's down the garden with Robin. Let's go while she's not looking our way. Dad would kill me if he knew I'd broken into your gran's barn.'

Of course Robin saw us and ran up the grass. 'Robin want Granny Lee. Granny look for holy bottle,' he was saying before his mother came up.

'Where have you *been*?' Mrs Gooding asked. 'I couldn't see you!' She was behaving as if we were toddlers who had to be kept in sight at all times.

'Making a camp in the willow,' Fay said quickly.

Robin looked at it and clung to his mother's hand. 'Don't like it. Rob won't go there.'

'Have you been teasing him again, Fay?' his mother asked.

'You know what happens if you tell tales,' Fay said angrily and Robin burst into tears.

I'd had enough. 'Got to go,' I said. 'Thanks for tea.' I heard Fay shouting and Robin crying as I hurried home.

When Mum asked me how I got on, I said, slowly: 'She's got all these dolls – dolls at her age! I feel sorry for her, though.' I tailed off.

At supper, Mum and Matthew talked about boring things like could they afford a new carpet and how all the rooms needed decorating. Jez was quiet, as usual, and I was trying to work out what might have happened to Gran.

Mum and Matthew had gone on to discuss where to put some furniture. I thought they'd finished so I blurted out: 'Hills thought that someone could have attacked Gran.' I didn't add she'd decided it wasn't possible.

Everyone looked startled and stared at me. 'Fran darling,' Mum said gently. 'I know you're missing her a lot but you've got to try to forget her death now. It was a terrible shock for us but we'll never know what happened. The police didn't find any trace of a break-in, and she hadn't any marks...' She paused, looking upset. 'Any signs of being hit on her body.'

I couldn't stop: 'That doesn't mean anything. She could have heard a noise, run out to the garden and tried to stop him taking the boat. Or – it could have been an argument – a row, when someone pushed her in the water and then ran off in a panic.' Should I tell Mum about Mr Gooding's threat? But already Matthew was looking at me and shaking his head slightly, as if to warn me to stop. He put his hand over Mum's, as if to steady her. Jez was staring at me – everyone was staring.

'Fran darling,' Mum said in a choky kind of voice, 'you're just upsetting yourself with all these ideas. I told you, they said at the inquest she'd had a heart attack – so it sounds just like an accident to me. Maybe she saw an injured duck or swan and got the boat out in a hurry to bring it in. You know how she often rescued sick creatures. Only the effort must have been too much for her. I wish we'd been to see her that weekend.' Mum looked at me and for a moment we were linked together with memories.

Matthew still held Mum's hand. 'Izzy darling, I thought we agreed not to talk about it?' He turned to me and spoke quite gently but firmly. 'Fran – we can't undo the past. We're trying to make a fresh start here. And everyone feels guilty when someone dies. You must wish so much you'd seen your granny that weekend and then she wouldn't have died. Death...' he murmured. 'There's always something you wish you'd done or hadn't done – things you wish you hadn't said...'

Suddenly I saw that Jez's face was almost contorted as he tried not to cry. I thought about his mother's climbing accident. Perhaps he felt if he'd been there...

It was then I felt sad for him as well as for myself, really sad. He made some excuse, refused pudding, taking an apple away to his room.

When we'd finished Matthew talked about a housework rota as he and Mum would both be working after this week: he's a librarian and she's a salesperson for Jeans Unlimited. 'Let's start as we mean to go on,' he suggested. 'Fran – could you please ask Jez to come and help now?'

When I went in, he was sitting at his computer again and I just had time to see he'd typed: *Grotty day unpacking – I miss home a lot. Izzy's not too bad. Fran is . . .*

'Your dad wants us to wash up,' I said.

He touched the keys and all I saw was the screensaver pattern. 'Dad loves organising,' he grumbled.

I felt sure he'd been going to type: *Fran is a nutcase* or *I don't like Fran*, so I said: 'You can't keep creeping off to your boring old computer.' I was actually jealous. I'd always secretly wanted one only Mum's pay didn't run to computers.

He swung round on his chair. 'Only boring if you're too thick to understand them.' His cold green eyes were scornful and his voice loud.

'You calling me thick?' I shouted. Then I ran downstairs and heard him following.

As I opened the kitchen door, Matthew was saying: 'It's early days, darling.' They were sitting very close together, holding hands like teenagers.

26

'We heard you two shouting at each other,' Mum said reproachfully.

I felt guilty. Gran wouldn't want me to make Mum unhappy. 'Sorry,' I said and started to wash up. Jez came to help but he didn't talk to me and he went back to his computer once we'd finished.

I took the dogs down the garden so they'd get to know each other. The evening was hot and still and Bas settled down under the apple tree, his face furrowed and drooping with worry. Do basset-hounds ever look happy? But I suppose he was homesick, like Jez. Sophie gave up trying to get him to play and followed me down to the river's edge.

The water is glowing with sunset light. I stare at it and wish my real dad was still alive. Gran's death has somehow unlocked a door I shut long ago. My eyes fill with tears. I remember, after all this time, the day he had the motor-bike accident – the police at the door and Mum crying out. Sophie was a puppy then and I'd just sat, hugging her.

Sophie whines and I see someone swimming towards me. Brown arms, churning a fast crawl...it's Denny! She treads water and waves. 'It's lovely in!' she calls.

I take off my jeans and trainers and dive in from our duckboard landing-stage. As I surface, I hear Sophie bark and a great splash as she comes after me. I smell the familiar muddy scent of the river water and feel the delicious silky coolness against my hot skin.

'Race you!' Denny says. I can just see her round face in the rapidly advancing dusk. We line up in the middle and I feel the tug of the current against my legs.

'Go!' she shouts and swims fast down river. Sophie barks as she dog-paddles behind us. We're passing the end of the Goodings' garden, Denny just ahead of me, when I hear Mum calling.

'You'd better go,' Denny pants. 'See you tomorrow.' She swims on while Sophie follows me back.

Mum, white-faced, is standing on the bank. 'Come in at once!' she shouts. 'Can't you keep away from the river? It's deep and the current's quite strong here. I don't think you should swim on your own, Fran. And look at you – with a sopping tee-shirt and wet pants! I'd have thought after yesterday...'

'I wasn't alone,' I say. 'There was this girl I know...'

Sophie interrupted by shaking herself all over Mum and Bas, just as Matthew and Jez appeared.

'She's been in that river,' Mum moaned. 'As if last night wasn't enough.'

Matthew put his arm round her. 'You said she was a good swimmer. But I think you might try to resist this fatal urge to get in or on the river, Fran dear, just at the moment. And you aren't exactly dressed for it.' He looked away and I saw he was trying to hide a smile.

Mega-embarrassed, I pulled my jeans over my wet legs as fast as I could. 'Gran and I always swim there and...' I trailed off. I was talking as if Gran were alive.

Mum's face looked very white in the dusk. I shivered.

'I've got the kettle on for tea,' Matthew said. 'Come on, Fran.' He put his hand on my arm but I moved away.

I went to change. When I came back into the kitchen I heard them talking. 'Maybe it would be a good idea, Izzy darling, if we all had a trip in that boat. I can't have you haunted like this,' Matthew was saying. 'If you faced up to it...'

She turned away, without speaking, pouring hot water on the tea bags. 'Perhaps on Fran's birthday.'

On my last birthday, Gran had been there, and we'd had a picnic by the river. I went to my room, trying not to cry and muffled myself with my Walkie, listening to loud pop music. They'd got each other and I was very alone. 'Oh Gran!' I muttered. 'Why did you have to die?' It sounds crazy but somehow I felt mad at her for leaving me.

There was a scratching at my door. I let Sophie in and she jumped up on my bed, first licking my face and then curling up heavily on my feet. She smelled of dog and of the river and I felt much better.

That night I dreamed I was drowning and Denny was laughing at me. I tried to call out but I couldn't make a sound. Then somehow I *was* Gran, in the river, my legs kicking at the clinging nightdress and I couldn't breathe or move. Fay's Green Woman head floated past me and I tried to hold on to it but it slid away. Then I saw Mum and Matthew in a boat and I tried to call out for help. They were holding hands and laughing and didn't see me...the water was over my head, dragging me down...

I was screaming and Mum was there. 'Darling, I thought you'd stopped nightmares.' She held me tight and I felt safe. She smelled of roses and her silky hair flopped against my neck. I wished time could stand still like this – just Mum and me together.

Chapter 4

The nightmare made me wake up even more determined to find out the truth about Gran's death. The more I thought about it, the more sure I became that Fay was protecting her father. Somehow, I had to put pressure on her.

I wanted to rush round and shake her, make her tell me but it wouldn't work. If her father bullied her, more bullying would just make her cry. Besides, I was really sorry for her.

After breakfast, Matthew, Jez and Bas drove off to stock up on food in the nearest town and Mum suggested I finished unpacking while she tried to sort out the mega pile of sheets and towels.

I chucked more things into drawers and stuck up some of my posters and photos of pop stars that I'd brought with me. Then I went along the landing to the linen cupboard. Mum was looking at an embroidered tablecloth. 'Apparently, Helen, Matthew's wife, was brilliant at needlework,' she said. 'It doesn't seem to go with being so athletic – mountain climbing and so on.'

'I expect she could do everything,' I said nastily. 'I bet she was Mrs Perfect.'

'Well, the way you talk your father was Mr Perfect,

wasn't he?' she snapped back unexpectedly. 'People's faults are often forgotten when they die.'

'Well, Gran didn't have any faults, did she?'

Mum smiled and glanced at me. 'Not really. Except she thought she could help the whole wide world and do it on her own.'

Like helping the Goodings and not confiding in anyone... Downstairs, Sophie whined, reminding us she hadn't had a walk.

'Why don't you take her for a walk?' Mum asked.

I thought about Gran's grave: none of us had gone there since the funeral. 'Can I take some flowers to Gran's grave?' On the way back, I'd think of a way of seeing Fay on her own.

'If it helps you, darling. I always feel flowers are for the living. Have a look round the garden.' She gave a desperate push to squeeze the last sheets in the cupboard, unfamiliar, dark blue sheets belonging to the Turners.

I went out into the ragged garden. The sky was heavy and grey and yet it was stickily warm. Nothing stirred when I walked under the apple tree. I picked a bunch of Michaelmas daisies and two of the sunflowers we'd sown by the barn. We both loved sunflowers because of their cheerful faces.

Sophie bounced along happily, pulling on her lead. The quickest way to the church was along the road, not through the woods.

As if she knew I wanted to see her – or as if she had

been watching out for me – Fay came out of her garden gate. Although it was so hot, she was wearing a long-sleeved pink dress with a white collar and cuffs; uncool was the word – literally! Sophie bounced delightedly at her and Fay smiled. 'I wish we had a dog,' she said, running her fingers through Sophie's black curly coat. 'Dad doesn't like them. He says they're unhygienic.' Surprise surprise! He didn't sound as if he liked anything much. She looked at the flowers. 'Where are you going? I'm off to the shop for Mum.'

I realised she was lonely and bored. She hadn't got a basket so I guessed she'd made up the shopping. 'I'm taking flowers to my gran's grave.'

Her face sort of twitched and she began to bite her almost invisible nails. 'I wish she hadn't died,' she muttered.

This was my chance. 'You know, if you saw something and didn't tell the police it would be a crime.' I tried to remember TV police dramas. 'It's called... aiding and betting or something like that.'

'Don't know what you're on about,' she muttered.

I pulled Sophie into the side as a car swooshed past us. 'If someone you knew scared Gran so she had a heart attack, you ought to tell. He couldn't hurt you afterwards if he was in prison.'

She was staring down at her old-fashioned sandals and white socks, walking slowly and deliberately like an old woman. Then she spoke fast and rather breathlessly. 'I did see a sinister sort of tramp that day. I was in the garden the evening before she died and I saw him walking along the river-path towards Folly Farm.'

'Why didn't you tell the police?'

'I was so upset after I forgot. Your gran was so kind she'd probably give him food and maybe he came back for money. And she said no so he hit her and then pushed her into the boat so people would think she'd had an accident and then sort of tipped her out.'

She had full marks for trying to invent a cover-up. Could her father have done this to Gran? 'He could only have scared her badly so she had a heart attack,' I said. 'Because they didn't find...' I had to stop.

'A push could knock over an old lady,' she said in a limp voice.

'Yes. Your Green Woman would want the truth, wouldn't she? Perhaps she'd punish you if you lied to me?'

'I'm not lying! You're horrible to me and I just want to be friends!' And she ran ahead of me down the lane.

I thought I'd done enough at the moment. And I could be wrong. I had to stay friends with her if I wanted to convince her that she needn't be loyal to her dad.

So I caught up with her, sweating in the sticky heat, Sophie delighted with the run. 'Sorry. I do want to be friends. You do look hot in that dress.'

'I burn easily.' She stopped and stared at me. 'You've not told on me, about the barn and the Green Woman?'

'No. But I think the barn's ours, really. They'll want to put things there.'

She gave a kind of gasp. 'I'll have to find somewhere else – could you please head them off for a bit?' She sounded so desperate that I said I'd try. 'It's mega important.' She must have seen my face because she went on. 'You think it's all kids' stuff, don't you? If my Green Woman made magic for you, then you'd believe.'

I felt sorry for her. 'I suppose I might.' I thought I'd go along with her games. 'Tell you what, make a spell so Jez asks to board at his posh old school instead of going to school with me.' I'd heard Matthew telling Mum the school took boarders.

'I'll ask her.' She was so ordinary about it – as if the Green Woman was real! 'It must be a pain to have a stepbrother – a real one's bad enough. Look – I've got a really creepy video – why not get away later on and see it with me?'

'I might.' It could be a chance to find out more.

When we came to the churchyard, Fay shivered and walked on to the shop without a word.

I let Sophie off the lead and found Gran's grave amongst the new ones.

I stared at the new tombstone. Underneath Gran's name and the dates were carved words: '*Do not stand by my grave and weep. I am not there...*' I cried as I filled the holder and stuck in the flowers.

Sophie was barking at the far side of the churchyard and I saw Denny jumping down from the wall where I'd first seen her. Sophie was bouncing up delightedly, licking her face.

She looked at the tombstone. 'Don't cry. I bet she wouldn't want you to.'

'But I miss her so much.' I sniffed.

She put her arm round me and I smelled cows and hay. 'I think you've got to sort of let her go.'

Before I could ask her what she meant I had to run off and catch Sophie, who'd been investigating the rubbish heap. She was rushing round the graveyard carrying a big red bow off some dead flowers. Denny ran after me, laughing loudly.

When I'd caught Sophie, I said: 'Was it you, on the barn roof?'

She smiled. 'I didn't mean to scare you both. I was just looking to see what Fay was up to. Candles are dangerous. I reckon she and her mum need help. Well, got to go – work to do.' She was off and over the wall before I could ask her what she meant about the Goodings.

Fay was waiting for me by the gate to the churchyard. She was carrying a plastic bag and looked very hot. Sophie greeted her like a long-lost friend and Fay actually smiled.

I decided to wait for a the right moment to talk to her again. 'Let's go back through the wood – Sophie needs a run,' I said.

'All right.' She was weighed down one side with her bag.

'Is it heavy? Tins or something?' I asked, just for something to say.

'Cat food. Dad takes us out to the supermarket but he'd not let me buy any. He doesn't like cats. I feed Obediah, you know. He still comes to the barn.'

So that was why I hadn't seen him much since we moved. I'd thought he was scared of Bas. We went through the gate into the wood and I let Sophie off the lead.

'I might get some more rowan,' Fay said. 'It's magic, you know. It protects you from evil.' She went up to a beech tree and stroked the bark. 'I like trees. I talk to them sometimes. The Green Woman's taught me that they listen. I tell them about my dad.'

The way she said it stopped me laughing at her. 'Why don't you tell someone real about your dad if he hurts you?' If he'd scared Gran I wanted him behind bars.

'I told you. Robin and I'd be taken away. Mum warned me. I don't want to live in a Home.'

'Wouldn't they just take him away? After all, he could hurt someone else . . .'

'Stop it! I'm not listening!' She ran off, the plastic bag banging against her legs and Sophie bounding at her side. Then Sophie was barking and running, right down the long ride. Stripes of shade and sun seemed to dazzle me but I thought I saw Denny. Then she was gone and so was Sophie.

Chapter 5

'I've got to go,' Fay said after we'd called Sophie for ages, until we were hoarse. 'Won't she find her way back?'

'I suppose she might.' I didn't know what to do. 'Let's go home and see.'

We met a couple walking their dog, but they hadn't seen Sophie. Fay hurried into her house. I walked into the kitchen where Jez and Matthew sat over the remains of lunch. 'Did Sophie come back?' I asked.

'No,' said Matthew. 'You've lost her?' I nodded miserably. 'Your mum's gone over to Mrs Gooding's. She rang up in an hysterical state saying Fay had been so long shopping that something terrible must have happened to her. Did Fay go with you, then? You're late enough yourself.'

'We were looking for Sophie.'

'Won't she find her way back?' Jez asked. 'Bas would.' He stroked the domed head. 'He can follow a scent.'

'She might – but she has to cross the road from the woods. A car could hit her.'

'Why not have something to eat and wait and see if Sophie turns up?' Matthew asked. He was making a

38

cheese sandwich as he talked. 'You must be thirsty.' He filled a tall glass with orange juice and ice. There was something soothing about him and the drink tasted wonderful.

Mum came in looking hot and cross. 'Fran! Mrs Gooding's been terribly upset because Fay was late and then the girl came in saying she'd been helping you look for Sophie in the woods. Her mother said she was never allowed in the woods anyway.' She paused for breath.

I was hot and tired. 'It wasn't my fault!' I almost shouted. 'She tagged along with me. And I'm going to look for Sophie now.' I flung down my sandwich and marched out. To my surprise, Jez and Bas caught up with me. 'Bas might scent her out,' he said. 'Show me where you last saw her.'

When we came to the place, Jez made encouraging noises. Bas sniffed at Sophie's lead, then circled the ground, his brows even more furrowed with concentration. He led us down a narrow track, past a grove of silver birch trees and along a thin path through brambles and bracken and the pink spires of fireweed, down towards the river. He bayed and was answered by Sophie's higher bark. Sophie ran out of a tangle of bushes, bouncing at Bas and shaking water all over us.

I jumped back, too late. 'Bas was brilliant!' I stroked his smooth head.

'They use bassets for hunting in France,' Jez said. He swiped at a cloud of midges. 'I'd better go. I come up in lumps with midge bites.' I thanked him for helping. 'It was a good chance to get away from the lovebirds!' He actually smiled and I liked him much better. 'Coming?'

'Yes – oh, Sophie!' The stupid dog was burrowing back into the bushes, whining and wouldn't listen to my calls. 'I'd better go after her.'

'I'll tell them you found her,' he called as he went.

I pushed through the thick leaves and found myself in a kind of den. A willow had fallen across the Dene's narrow tributary forming one wall and someone had made a rough fence, weaving willow twigs through upright sticks. Sophie whined at Denny, who was walking barefoot across the fallen trunk, waving at me as she balanced rather unsteadily.

'She wouldn't leave me,' she said. 'She followed me here. Then she tried to walk along the tree trunk and fell in so I dried her with my shirt. I told her to go home but she wouldn't.'

'Is this your den?'

'Yes – Denny's Den!' She laughed and jumped down beside me. 'Look!' She pointed at a flash of brilliant blue, flying down river. 'Kingfisher!'

I was pleased. 'We looked last summer but Gran said she thought maybe there weren't any kingfishers here now.' I hesitated. Then I thought of the tramp. I was almost sure Fay had made him up but I could check with Denny. 'Fay says she saw a tramp hanging around near Folly Farm the evening before my gran died. Did you see him?'

She hesitated. 'I wasn't there, that evening. Poor

Fay...' she began but stopped. Someone was calling my name.

'It's Matthew – he must have come after me. I'd better go. See you!' I plunged back through the bushes, this time with Sophie safely on the lead.

Jez and his father were coming down the narrow track. Matthew actually smiled at me. 'There you are! I came to help but Jez said you'd found Sophie.'

He was so keen to get home he walked slightly ahead of us and Jez grumbled quietly: 'He wants us to help in the garden, though it's so hot. Dad just doesn't feel the heat. Mum used to say he must have lizard-skin, loving the sun so much. She was more like me. But she'd not mind the cold, even when she was rock climbing.'

We were actually having a conversation! 'My gran was a bit like that. More of an outdoor type than Mum.'

'You stayed here with her, didn't you?'

'Yes. It helped when Mum was working. And Gran came to us last Christmas.' As I said the words I could see us, laughing over silly card games and Gran so happy and well. 'Then I stayed a week at Easter while Mum went on that holiday – when she met your dad.' And they came back engaged to be married. It had been a shock. Why did they have to be so quick? To my horror I found tears sliding down my cheeks. Matthew was calling us to hurry up.

'Fran's got something in her eye,' Jez said, surprising me again.

Matthew said he'd look at it when we got back.

41

'Thanks,' I said again to Jez, wiping my face.

'I wish I could cry – about Mum,' he said and then relapsed into his usual silence.

A good thing about my mum is that she's too bubbly to be cross for long. 'Oh, you found Sophie. Good!' she said. 'Now, eat up your sandwiches, Fran. We've got lots to do in the garden this afternoon.'

I heard the telephone ringing when we were all sweating away at the weeding and ran inside; any excuse to stop. It was Hills. 'Fran! I've looked out those old snaps. How about popping in for tea next Tuesday? I think you need to talk about your granny's death.'

She was dead right! I wanted to find evidence against Mr Gooding and send him to prison. Perhaps Hills could help me. 'Tuesday's fine,' I said.

'Good.' She paused and cleared her throat. 'Maybe you didn't know that your gran told me she was going to baby-sit for the Goodings the night before she died? I wondered afterwards if something had happened – maybe someone breaking in when she was out? It was all such a shock that I never said anything to your mother and I just couldn't ring up the police. Then I heard she'd died early in the morning, not in the night so my idea didn't seem likely. Of course I don't know if your gran did baby-sit in the end. Mrs Gooding's nerves were too bad to come to the inquest and her husband was away. Anyway, perhaps you can find out more.'

When I put the phone down, I wondered why the

42

Goodings hadn't said anything about that evening? Did they think it would upset me? Fay must have been lying when she said she didn't remember. Could there have been some kind of row when the Goodings came back from their evening out? Maybe Gran had threatened to report Mr Gooding to the police and he'd crept round, early, and caused her heart attack? Should I tell Mum? But she'd say we hadn't any proof, and we hadn't – not yet.

It was boiling hot and after another hour's weeding, we all collapsed in the shade of the big apple tree at tea-time, knocking back apple juice, Coke, water, anything wet!

Jez sat by Matthew. 'It's as hot as that day when we were camping in France, isn't it, Dad?' he said. 'Do you remember, we slept outside, under the stars.'

'Until that French bullock came over and woke us up!' Matthew laughed. 'And your mum chased it off. She loved camping – the meals she used to cook up on that little stove!'

'Helen's Hash,' Jez said dreamily.

'I made Matthew's Mush but nobody liked it!' He laughed and Jez joined in. Their conversation made me feel totally alien. It was like opening a book in the middle when you don't know all the characters. Or your parents talking about before you were born.

'We tried camping once and I hated it,' Mum said. 'Fran had a tummy-bug and it was about a hundred miles to the loo and it rained every day.'

'I can remember Dad going off to get crisps and Cokes and getting lost on the way back from the pub so you were worried.'

'Yes,' Mum said thoughtfully. 'I remember. I don't think he was lost.'

I wondered what she meant but Matthew was rousing us to go back to work and I joined in Jez's protests. 'Far too hot!' we said and Matthew eventually agreed. So it was back to stacking bookshelves and unpacking the last of the boxes.

'Where's Obediah?' Mum asked. 'I've hardly seen him since we came.'

'I think he goes back to the Goodings. He's not used to Bas,' I explained.

Mum looked worried. 'That won't do, if Mr Gooding doesn't like cats.'

'He's away a lot,' I said. I wanted to talk to her about the way he treated Fay but I had promised not to. I didn't know much about the law and perhaps Fay was right and the authorities would take Fay and Robin away.

At supper, the talk drifted to going back to school in September. 'Fallowfield is big but it's really quite a good comprehensive,' Mum said. 'We went to see it before we moved. Of course, Jez has to register there yet.'

He looked up. 'I don't really want to change schools. Dad – they take some boarders at my old school, don't they?'

I felt my face go hot. I'd challenged Fay to work some magic...Now Jez was doing what I'd jokingly suggested. He wanted to board! Just as I was getting to know him, too.

Matthew sighed. 'We can't afford it. Sorry.' So that was the end of my plan. I decided to make a great effort to cheer Jez up after supper, while we washed up together.

'The school looks okay,' I said. 'There's a huge science lab and masses of people go on to university.'

Jez's glasses had steamed up so he took them off. 'Yeah – it isn't that. It's well, strange here and I'm used to my old school. Being there helped me after Mum died, somehow. It was kind of fixed, safe, when everything else was falling apart. And here, now Dad's married your mother...' He stopped but I got the drift. He was going to say he wasn't happy here. Well, he could *try* more.

'My mum's a great person,' I said defensively. 'Like my gran was.' I returned a plate still gummed-up with macaroni cheese. 'Use the brush on the plate.'

'Bossy, aren't you!' He scrubbed at the plate, then put it down without looking. It slipped off, breaking on the stone floor. He swore loudly – yes, quiet Jez actually swore! – and picked up the pieces, cutting his finger. He wrapped a drying-up cloth round it but the blood came through, staining it quickly.

Mum and Matthew were trying to organise the sitting-room so I fetched the First Aid box. 'I'll do it,' Jez said but it was his right hand and a deep little cut. I'd done a Junior First Aid course and blood didn't worry me. I managed to bandage his finger and felt rather pleased with the result. When Mum came in, though, she got all wound-up and insisted on undoing my careful work. 'It needs antiseptic,' she said.

'It was a clean plate,' I said because poor Jez looked really embarrassed at all the fuss.

Later on, I was sitting on my bed, trying to fit together in my mind all the little bits I'd heard about Gran's death, when a blast of organ music thundered through the wall. I banged on Jez's door. 'It's too loud!' I shouted. He took no notice so I went in.

He turned round and I saw that he'd been sticking an enlarged colour photo on the wall with Blu-tack. It was of a slim woman, dressed for climbing, standing on a rock. Her ginger curls were blown by the wind and she was laughing.

'My mum,' he said, above the music.

This wasn't the moment to complain. 'She's pretty.'

'She was. Did you want something?" I mumbled about the music and he turned it down. 'Sorry.'

I suddenly wondered if he could help me find out about Gran. Or would he laugh at me, playing detective? I was just going to say something when there was a knock at the door and Mum came in to see if Jez's hand was still bleeding. 'Matthew thinks I'm fussing but I think it could have done with a stitch.'

'It's okay,' Jez mumbled, again looking mega-embarrassed.

'Time for bed, Fran,' Mum said as she went out and I

could have killed her. After all, Jez was only a year older than me.

'My mother never worried about cuts and things,' he said. 'When I was little, I was told not to cry if I fell over.'

It figured, his hearty, rock-climbing mother being tough on crying and I felt a bit sorry for him. My mum had always given me a great hug if I fell over when I was little.

That night, as I tried to sleep I kept thinking of Gran in the river. Then Fay's nightmare pictures ran through my mind as if on video. Could her Green Woman really help her make spells? Already Jez had wanted to board at school, hadn't he? And he'd hurt his hand. No, I was being as silly as Fay herself.

And none of this was as important as making Mr Gooding tell me what happened when Gran died.

Chapter 6

I dreamed Jez was dead, floating on the dark river water.
He lay on his back with his glasses on and his arms out-
stretched. Somehow I had killed him. I was in the boat –
Gran's boat – with Fay. 'We've got to get him out,' I said
but she laughed as she rowed past him. I leaned out of the
boat and tried to reach for Jez but he disappeared and I
was staring at the bobbing head of the Green Woman.

This time I didn't scream but the dream lingered after
I woke up. Perhaps it was a sign that there really was
something magic about Fay's Green Woman.

It didn't help when Jez looked pale and tired at
breakfast and ate with his left hand. He said his finger
hurt quite a bit. Mum suggested Matthew took him to
the doctor's, as they were going to the do-it-yourself
shop in town anyway.

I wanted to talk to Fay – then ask more people in the
village about Gran and whether they'd seen the tramp.
But as soon as Matthew and Jez had gone, Mum nagged
me into tidying my room and finishing unpacking my
clothes.

I was just kicking some of my rubbish under the bed
when the doorbell rang and Mum called up that Fay was
there to see me.

This was just what I wanted! I ran downstairs. Fay was actually wearing a faded long-sleeved shirt and jeans with holes in the knees instead of her old-fashioned clothes. 'Coming round?' she asked. Mum asked how her mother was.

'Oh, she's fine. Half-asleep as usual. Took extra tranks. after yesterday.' She smiled at Mum. 'Could you spare Fran? I get so bored and lonely when Mum's resting and Robin's asleep. We've got loads in the freezer if she wants to eat.'

I told Mum I'd more or less finished my room and I'd help her when I got back and she let me go, rather reluctantly. 'How come the old jeans?' I asked Fay when we were outside. 'You're usually all dressed up.'

She actually laughed. 'I keep these hidden away for when my dad's not there and Mum's zonked out. I bought them at the church jumble.'

So she could be quite normal, if she was allowed.

I had to talk to her about Jez. 'Look – you know you said your Green Woman put spells on people? I suppose it's just coincidence but Jez asked to go to boarding school last night.'

She looked happy. 'There you are! She listens to me like I said. Is he going?'

'No. There's not enough money. And today he's at the doctor's – he cut his finger.' I hesitated. 'Did your Green Woman do that?'

'I told you – she only does good magic.' She lowered her voice. 'Mustn't wake up my mum,' she whispered.

'I'd better see if Robin's still asleep. I'm meant to keep an eye on him when Mum's poorly. He'd be all right if Mum didn't smother him and Dad didn't...' She didn't finish but went upstairs while I waited in the hall.

She came back looking worried. 'He's not there! I'd better look in the garden. Mum's dead asleep.'

There was a toy truck by the willow tree.

'He's there – in my magic place!' she shouted furiously as she ran. 'I thought I'd taught him a lesson last time!'

I followed her through the curtain of willow leaves and the door into the barn. Robin was singing tunelessly, sitting in front of Fay's altar, cuddling the head of the Green Woman. Obediah was curled beside an empty saucer.

'Put her down!' Fay yelled, running forward.

Robin dropped the head and started to cry. Obediah sensed trouble and ran out of the gap under the barn door, leading to our garden.

'Don't...' I began and then there was a great thump on the roof. I looked up. A brown hand was pushing through the space in the tiles. The next minute Fay was reeling back with mud splattered all over her face! She gave a strangled shout and ran outside, shouting something. Robin was howling so I picked him up and followed her.

Denny was on the barn roof, her sturdy legs braced on either side of the ridge. 'You leave him alone!' she called down.

'What's it to do with you?' Fay asked, peering upwards and wiping mud off her face. 'What are you doing on my roof?'

'It's not your roof – it's our barn,' I said. 'And it's my friend, Denny. She lives near here. She's right, Fay. You shouldn't have a go at Robin. He was really scared.' I put him down but he clung to my legs, crying. Fay ran back into the barn.

'Robin!' Denny called down. 'Don't cry.' He looked up at her and waved, smiling through his tears.

'Meet you by the river later on?' Denny said as she scrambled off the roof, running down the garden and through the gate to the river. Robin tried to follow her but I held him. He felt so fragile and bird-boned – how could Fay get mad at him? He sucked his thumb while he clutched his pink handkerchief. I found stones and twigs to put in his little truck and he soon joined in and stopped crying, so I went to find Fay.

She was sitting cross-legged in front of the altar. She'd put the Green Woman's head back and lit the candles. 'You're horrible to poor Robin!' I said angrily. 'He's only little.'

She looked up at me. 'You don't know what it's like to have a baby brother messing up your things. I wanted to help Mum with him when he was tiny but Dad shouted at me. He said I might drop him.' The candlelight gleamed on the tears running down her face.

'Look – about the magic.' I stared at the black eye sockets of the Green Woman. The lump of driftwood

51

seemed to change as I looked, becoming more like a head all the time. 'If he can't board, I don't want Jez to go away. I don't want anything weird to happen to him. He's okay really.'

'I told her you wanted him to go,' Fay said, in a funny, sing-song voice. 'She listens to me and then she does magic.'

'Well, tell her to stop, then.' Did I believe in the magic now? The Green Woman's twisted mouth seemed to smile. It was just a slit in the wood and yet...

'If I can,' Fay said dreamily.

I wanted to shake her. Then I remembered what I was going to ask her. 'Why didn't you tell me Gran came to baby-sit for your mum that night – before she died?'

Fay went on staring at the Green Woman. 'I didn't think it was important.'

'Did anything happen that evening?'

'No.'

I didn't believe her. 'Tell me! Did Gran have a row with your dad?' I gripped her shoulders and shook her gently.

She gave a kind of scream. 'It hurts! I don't know. He walked her back home: I heard them go.'

I let go her shoulders. 'Did you get sunburnt or something?' I asked her. 'Is that why you always wear long sleeves?'

She was shaking as she crossed her arms protectively across her body. As if I might hit her... 'Stop it! Stop it!' she screamed, pulling away and running off.

I blew the candles out and followed her outside, where she was staring down at Robin with a funny expression on her face.

'Fay, Robin!' Mrs Gooding was standing outside the back door. 'Come in!'

Fay wiped her tears away with the back of her hand as her mother picked Robin up. 'I did ask you to tell me when he woke, Fay,' she said reproachfully. 'Look at the dirt on him! It's a good thing your father isn't here.'

We followed her inside.

'Nasty Fay cross with Robin,' he said in a special baby voice, patting his mum's face with muddy hands.

'Isn't she a naughty sister then?' Mrs Gooding murmured to him. 'Fay – he's only three!'

'I bet you told me off when I was three!' Fay glowered at her mum. 'It's all Robin, Robin. You never think about me!'

'Of course I do,' her mum said. Bowed under Robin's weight, she sank into a kitchen chair. 'But you're growing up and Robin still needs me.'

Fay changed then, patting her mother on the shoulder and offering to get our lunch. Her mother took some pills out of her pocket. 'No, Mum. Dad's not here. You don't need them.'

Mrs Gooding obediently put the pills back. 'You're right, Fay dear. I shall get dressed.'

I felt very sorry for Fay. No wonder she had to escape to her Green Woman.

We had pizzas and ready-made milk shakes. Mrs

Gooding's hand trembled a little as she ate hers but she asked me the usual boring things adults think they must – about school, and what did I want to be when I grew up.

At last I managed to get a word in: 'About my gran – was she okay when she baby-sat for you the night before she died?'

Mrs Gooding's pale face flushed and her voice trembled. 'She seemed quite well. I gather she'd had a little bother with Robin but...' She began to cry, silently and Fay glared at me.

'You'd better go,' she hissed, so I did.

Matthew's car was back and I heard laughter in the garden. I went through the side entrance and saw Mum wearing her bikini, giggling like a kid as Matthew ran after her with the hose on. I felt myself going red. Jez, his hand re-bandaged, came out of the back door just as Matthew cornered Mum by the barn door and turned the spray on full. 'Like kids, aren't they?' he said disapprovingly. We stood there, feeling embarrassed, then turned to go inside, away from the freakish sight.

'How's your hand?' I asked.

'Had to have two stitches and an antibiotic injection,' he was saying when we smelled the burning.

I found a blackened cake in the oven

'It's your birthday cake, Fran,' Mum wailed when I'd fetched them in to view the wreckage. Her slim body glistened with water and I noticed she'd painted her toe-nails red. It was mega-embarrassing with her standing there in her bikini. Luckily Jez had gone in the garden.

'I don't need a cake at my age,' I said.

'Poor old lady!' Matthew laughed. He had his hairy arm round my mum's waist.

I couldn't bear it. 'Sophie needs a walk.' I went out quickly.

I heard Mum calling me but I took no notice. I hurried Sophie along to the wood. I had to see Denny again; I wanted to talk to someone and she was so friendly and sensible. It was hotter than ever today and flies buzzed round my head as I went down the track to the river.

The den is empty. I sit on the fallen willow, dangling my feet above the water, hoping she'll come. I suddenly feel very alone. I try not to cry as I watch the shifting pattern of the willow leaves reflected in the water. Dragonflies shimmer over yellow water-lilies. A moorhen clacks and flies up. Then I see a spark of bright blue, zig-zagging from one bank to another. Sophie stands up and barks.

'Did you see the kingfisher again?' Denny is there, clambering along the willow trunk from the opposite bank. She sits down beside me. Bits of straw are stuck to her old shirt and her knees are streaked with dirt. 'What's the matter?'

'I'll never get used to Matthew and Mum. Maybe Jez isn't so bad but...'

'Give Matthew a chance.' She smiles. 'As my mum says – Rome wasn't built in a day. You've got to get to know him.'

I know she's right, really, but I just grunt. 'And I'm worried about Fay,' I go on. 'When you threw the mud perhaps you saw that lump of driftwood on a sort of altar. She calls it the Green Woman and thinks it can do magic. I told her I wanted Jez to go away and she's made a spell and he's hurt his hand . . . ' The words come out in a jumble.

I feel the warmth of Denny's brown hand on my arm. 'I guessed she'd got to you, when I spied you in the barn. She can't tell what's real and what isn't and she's sort of hiding in the magic from her dad. I guess he's really cruel to her. I've heard shouting and Fay screaming. We've got to help her somehow.'

At that moment, Sophie whines and disappears through the bushes, the way we've come. I call her but she takes no notice.

'Wait for me, Denny. I must get her.' I push back through the bushes. Sophie is prancing round Bas. Jez must be quite near. Suddenly I don't want him to meet Denny. She is my special friend and he'll probably laugh at her old clothes and thick country accent. I wait a moment but I can't see him, so I take both dogs back into the den but Denny has gone. Sophie sniffs at the tree-bridge and suddenly plunges in the river, swimming to the opposite bank. Bas stands on the bank and whines.

The bushes rustled and Jez thrust his way through. 'So this is where Bas got to,' he said. 'Why's your dog in the river?'

56

'Maybe chasing a duck or something.' Sophie was sniffing about on the opposite bank, where the willow-trunk bridge ended. I called her sharply. She whined rather sadly and then swam back, getting up the slithery bank with some difficulty. We jumped away as she shook water all over us.

Jez laughed at Sophie. 'You're a menace, you are!' Then he looked round the little den. I suddenly saw it through his eyes: just a muddy corner of the riverbank. 'I used to hide out in places like this when I was a kid.'

I felt irritated. He wasn't all that much older than me. 'Why did you follow me?'

'I guess they want to be alone together.' He sighed and ran his fingers through the curly wool on Sophie's head. Bas immediately moved up and leant heavily against his legs. 'You're jealous, aren't you?' Jez stroked him. Then he looked at the water. 'The river at the bottom of our garden's much wider, isn't it?'

'This is a tributary of that river, the Dene,' I said. 'The main river divides just above Folly Farm and this bit sort of wanders round the woods. Then the Dene splits again at the weir.'

'I wonder if there are any kingfishers?'

Just for a moment I was tempted. But I still wanted to keep Denny for myself and Jez would be back if I said I'd seen kingfishers. I said: 'They're pretty rare, you know. Hadn't we better get home?'

'Oh, all right. But I might come back. I know a bit about birds,' he said.

And on the way back he talked about going bird-spotting with Matthew – in fact, he got quite enthusiastic, for Jez. I could see what he might be like if he could settle down with us and stop comparing Mum with his mother.

Chapter 7

'I can't think why you ran off like that,' Mum said yet again. She gave me one of her motherly, appealing looks. Jez was off on his bike to get some things from the shop – so he said but I thought he was as fed up with unpacking as I was.

Matthew was plumbing-in the washing-machine – leaving us mere women to go on with the endless sorting and putting things away.

The afternoon stretched on, hot and boring. When Mum gave me empty cardboard containers to flatten, I jumped on them with all my pent-up longing for Gran – and anger with her 'murderer'.

The doorbell rang. I heard Mum talking, then she came back with Fay and Robin. 'Their daddy's asked if we could have them while he took their mummy to the hospital. She's had a little fall.' She was obviously talking in this babyish way for Robin, who looked tearful.

'Where's Granny Lee?' Robin asked, looking round the room.

'Oh – shut up, Robin!' Fay said irritably. Mum and Matthew stared at her and she bit her nails.

I agreed with her. I wanted to shout: 'She's dead!'

Instead I said, jerkily: 'She's gone. Gone to Heaven.'
Did I believe that?

Mum swung him onto her lap, in the kitchen chair.
'How about a bikkie?' she asked in a yukky voice. I
realised with a lurch that she and Matthew might have a
baby. Nothing will ever be the same.

Mum was stroking Robin's long fair hair when he
suddenly yelped. I turned round from making the tea
and saw her sweep back his fringe. There was a new-
looking bruise on his forehead. 'How did he do that?'
Mum asked.

'Fell over, didn't you, Rob?' Fay said quickly.

'Yeah,' and he sucked his thumb, clutching his pink
hanky. Mum took him off to watch the newly plugged-
in TV.

'Dad just got back,' Fay said dully. 'We didn't expect
him. He got really mad when he saw me in my old
jeans.'

'Why?' I asked, sorry for her.

'Mum says his work's not going well. Then he drinks.
Then he gets mad – at anything.'

At that moment, the doorbell rang again and Matthew
came back with Hills and Jez, who had a messy graze on
his face and torn jeans. Hills said there had been an
accident. 'I don't think it was my fault,' she said. 'It was
near the shop. He swerved to my side of the road and I
braked but my bonnet just hit his bike.'

Matthew made Jez sit down and sip a glass of water.
'It was a cat – ran right out in front of me,' he said. 'A

black cat.' I thought about Obediah but he'd always been a home-lover and didn't roam far.

Mum, hearing voices, came in and immediately fetched cotton wool and disinfectant. Jez protested but she firmly mopped at the graze.

'We've got the bicycle in my boot,' Hills said. 'Anyway, no bones broken.' But she looked shaken and Mum gave her a cup of tea.

Matthew went to get the bike. 'A bit too much for me to mend,' he said. 'Sorry, Jez, but I think you'll have to help pay for the repairs. The back wheel's buckled. Brake, next time, not swerve, or you could be killed. And were you wearing your helmet?'

'No.'

I noticed Fay was almost as pale as Jez and I thought about the Green Woman's spells.

'Can't we pay for the repairs?' Mum said. 'Poor old Jez – he's had a cut finger and now this.' I must say, for once I agreed with her.

'No. He has to learn,' Matthew said, unsmiling.

Hills, sensing family argument, went home, after reminding me about coming to see her the following week. Suddenly the dogs went to the back door, barking. We could hear Robin screaming, somewhere outside.

Fay shot out and we all followed. She grabbed her brother as he stood on the very edge of the riverbank. He struggled and shouted: 'Want bottle!' He was rather strangely pointing at the boat, which had again come loose and was drifting slowly downstream.

'He must have untied it!' Matthew was taking off his sandals. 'And I did a reef knot.'

'I'll get it.' I kicked my shoes off and jumped in, thankful I'd changed into shorts. Two strokes and I caught the trailing rope and brought the boat back. Fay was clutching Robin, muttering angrily at him. Matthew smiled and thanked me and he tied the boat securely to the iron ring. Mum was looking upset again.

'It's a good thing the boat did break loose or Robin might have got into it,' I pointed out and we all fell silent, thinking of Gran's 'accident'. Fay in particular was dead white and looked as if she might cry. As we went inside Robin went on about his 'holy bottle' so I asked her what he meant. 'Did it have holy water in it?'

'No, stupid! It was part of a child's hot-water bottle with a hole in it. He always had to take it to bed. Then he – lost it.' Why was her voice quiet and shaky? 'So he has a hanky now instead.'

Supper was ready early so Fay and Robin ate with us. Robin went to sleep on my mum's lap, clutching his pink hanky.

'By the way, you two,' Mum said. 'We've ordered a bookshelf and it will arrive on Monday, when we're back at work – so I'm afraid one of you will have to stay in for it.' She looked at Matthew. 'Hope you've got the cash – the man won't take a cheque.'

'Here – eighty, wasn't it?' Matthew gave Mum some notes and she put them in an envelope.

'You'll find it here, behind Gran's old kitchen clock,' she told us.

Matthew and Jez went out to see what could be done about the bike. Mum asked Fay and me to wash up while she kept an eye on Robin, who'd gone back to the TV.

Fay was rubbing her eyes. 'I've got ever such a headache,' she said. 'Must have been the shock of seeing Robin on the riverbank like that. Could you get me something for it?'

When I came back from the bathroom, she was slowly washing a plate.

'Sorry I haven't done much yet,' she said in a faint voice. 'But I felt rather funny.' Of course I had to tell her not to bother and I clattered away at the sink while she sat down and took the pills.

'What about Jez – hurting his finger and this accident on his bike...' I dug away at a sticky bit of batter. 'You said your Green Woman only did good spells, didn't you?'

'Of course. And sometimes she doesn't help.' She rubbed at her arm, pushing up the loose sleeve of her tee-shirt. I thought I saw small bruises, like fingermarks.

'Did your dad hurt you?' I asked.

She pulled down her sleeve and looked away. 'What I told you about Dad was a lie. Just forget it,' she said in a breathless, hurried sort of voice. 'Just my stupid little brother, grabbing my arm. I had to get him to bed and he wouldn't come.'

I didn't believe her. Surely little Robin couldn't have made those marks? Her dad must be threatening her not to tell.

Her voice changed. 'About the spells – you ought to be grateful. If your stepbrother boards after all, we can go on the bus to school together. I can tell you which gangs to watch out for.'

I wondered if anyone liked poor Fay at school; she would be an oddball, a weirdo. I would rather be friends with Denny. She looked a bit younger than me so perhaps she was in her last year at Junior School.

'I wish your Green Woman could tell me what happened to my gran,' I said.

'I told you – she wants you to forget,' Fay said in a silly, faraway voice. 'Don't you believe me about the tramp?'

Should I tell her I didn't believe in her tramp? But it was useless; she'd still defend her father. I had to wait for the right moment. 'You've not lost a special gran, have you?' I snapped. 'And I shall remember her even more, going on a picnic in the boat for my birthday, just as we did last year with her.'

'In the boat?' She stared at me. 'After what happened to your gran?'

'Mum doesn't want to but Matthew thinks it might help her to face up to Gran's death.' I remembered what I wanted to ask her. 'Why did Robin think his "holey bottle" was in the boat?' I asked. 'Did she ever take you both out in it?'

'No!' She thumped down a pile of plates. 'I can't swim. I hate the water. And Robin's only a baby. He doesn't know what he's saying.' The doorbell rang. 'Dad!' Fay began to bite her non-existent nails.

'I hope they've behaved themselves.' Mr Gooding's voice was cold and clear, like his pale blue eyes, eyes which fixed on Fay and me as if he'd caught us doing something wrong. He seemed to fill the room with his height and breadth, like the giant in Fay's picture.

Robin was holding my mum's hand and sucking his thumb fiercely. 'You're too old for that!' His father yanked the little boy's thumb out of his mouth and Robin began to cry, low, forlorn sobs, running to hide his face against my mother's legs.

She stared fiercely at Mr Gooding. 'He's been very good. I think he's a lovely little boy. And Fay's been helping Fran. How's your wife? Did she have a fall?'

He gave a sneering half-smile. 'She tripped over one of Robin's toys on the stairs. Never gets him to put things away. And of course the doctors say she has bad nerves – I tell her she ought to pull herself together, chuck away the pills, get a job. These days the doctors are far too soft with people like her.'

'It's not her fault, Dad,' Fay burst out. 'It's yours! You shout at her and...' She tailed off as he glared at her.

'You insolent little...' He pulled Robin out of Mum's arms. 'You'll go straight up to your room when we get home, young madam!' Robin was screaming as he dragged them both out of the house.

Mum exploded: 'He's absolutely dreadful! No wonder his wife's like that and as for those poor children...I wish there was something we could do.'

Was this the time to tell her she was right and that Fay's father hit his children and probably his wife too? I didn't believe in his story of Mrs Gooding's fall, either. But if we got him into trouble for hitting his children They might take Fay and Robin away – and also, I'd lose my chance to get him to confess about Gran. I wanted him to be put in prison for years and years!

When Matthew and Jez came in she told them what she thought. 'I wish we could help them.' She looked really upset.

He hugged her. 'I don't think we can interfere without proof. And it's up to Mrs Gooding herself to report her husband. She may not want to.'

He smiled at me and changed the conversation. 'Thirteen tomorrow, Fran! All we need is good weather for our picnic. I'm looking forward to it.'

Chapter 8

I tossed about all night, dreaming, and woke up half-smothered by fur. 'Obediah!' I muttered. Sophie was sprawled over my feet. I felt warm and safe with the animals. I didn't want to move.

Then with a jolt, I remembered my birthday – and the picnic. Mum said I'd been born at 4 a.m. so I was now thirteen. A teenager – most people at school wanted to be older but I wanted to stay the same. Exams, jobs, boyfriends – I didn't want any of them. I liked being me, now – or I had, until recently.

Again the rising sun was drawing a white mist from the river and something moved on the bank. Was it Denny? I dressed quickly and went downstairs, leaving Obediah curled peacefully on my bed.

Bas was in his basket in the kitchen but he followed Sophie and me into the garden. The dew-wet grass felt great under my bare feet. Sophie bounded ahead and nosed at something by the river's edge. Bas, now her adoring admirer, trailed after her. She came running back holding a strange-looking garland in her mouth.

It was carefully made out of scarlet and dark purple berries, twined together with reeds and somehow I knew I had to put it round my neck. Had Denny left it for me? I looked up and down the river but I couldn't see a swimmer and the dreaded boat was still tied up to the iron ring.

'Bare feet?' Mum said as I came into the kitchen. 'You've left wet marks all over the floor. And what's that round your neck?'

'Present from the river,' I said lightly and then wished I'd not because she looked away. I knew her so well. She must be dreading the picnic.

Matthew came in and put a carefully wrapped parcel by my plate. 'Happy birthday, Fran!' he said and gave me a quick hug, as if I might bite him. 'Wearing a magic garland to celebrate?' he asked. 'You must have got up early to find all those elder and rowan berries. I didn't know there was a rowan tree in the garden.'

'What do you mean?'

'Rowan has always been a magic tree – to protect people and places against evil and the elder is a magic plant too.'

Trust Matthew to know it all! But then I thought that perhaps Denny had given me this necklace of berries to protect me against horrible Mr Gooding as well as Fay's spells.

'Mind those berries don't fall in your cereal bowl!' Jez was smiling. I was just going to snap at him when he gave me a small parcel. 'Happy birthday. Aren't you going to undo your presents?'

He had given me a CD of Spanish guitar music. 'Thought you might like to try something different,' Jez said.

'Thanks,' I said, and meant it. Another surprise was a camera from Matthew and Mum. Up to now, we'd shared my dad's old one, which hadn't been up to much. Matthew got quite excited, showing me how it worked, and I must say, I was pleased.

'Brilliant,' I said. 'I've always wanted one of my own.'

'Matthew suggested it,' Mum said.

A nasty, sneaky thought came to me that yet again he was trying hard to be a Good Stepfather but even so, it was nice of him to think of it.

Mum had also given me a pair of red jeans. 'That's to spare us the black grunge clothes today! Try not to swim in them!' She laughed.

The thought of swimming seemed to trigger off Jez's wheezes – or maybe it was Obediah stalking into the kitchen. He went to fetch his inhaler. I thought hopefully they might put the picnic off.

Matthew frowned. 'Jez hasn't been as bad as this before. Must be the cat.' He exchanged fierce looks with Obediah, who immediately jumped on his lap. Cats always know how to get at people they don't like.

'Perhaps he doesn't want to go on the river picnic,' I muttered.

'That might be it,' Mum said quickly. 'As you know, I'm not so keen. How about the woods instead?'

Matthew held her hand and somehow I felt it was right, this time. 'We won't go in the boat if you really hate the idea, Izzy darling. But as I've said, it's probably

69

the best way to face your mother's death.'

I wondered if he could be right. If Mum could face the boat and the place where Gran's body was found, she might be able to talk about it, and stop shutting it away in a dark cupboard marked Death.

Fay came round then. She gave me a lump of wood on a string like hers and Robin handed me a tube of Smarties.

'I think he's eaten some of them,' Fay said. 'Why're you wearing that thing round your neck? Those elderberries and the rowan? I've just given you a piece of rowan wood to wear like mine, to keep off evil and death. You don't need that thing as well.'

'It's from my friend Denny,' I said defiantly. I wished I'd seen her because I could have asked her to come with us.

'That mucky-looking girl.' She looked disgusted. 'She's a spy – not a friend. I'm your friend.' Her eyes seemed huge as she stared at me. 'Dad says I've got to go now to help with the supermarket shopping. Come on, Robin.' As she went out, I saw red marks on the backs of her bare legs. Had she been going through brambles or...?

Mum heard the front door close. 'Oh, I was going to ask if she could picnic with us. There wouldn't be room for Robin but...'

I explained why Fay had to get back. 'That poor child has a difficult time,' Mum said. 'I still think we could help somehow.'

Jez came with us, wheezing slightly. 'I hate being left out because of this crappy asthma,' he muttered to me.

I'd always been pretty healthy but now I tried to imagine myself as Jez. I'd hate not to be able to breathe properly and I knew how cruel other kids at school could be if you'd got something wrong with you.

We left the dogs in the old stable with the half door open for air, as it was a mega-hot day, although by now the sun was hidden by dark grey clouds.

'Going to be a thunderstorm, I bet,' Jez said. 'I like storms.'

'Fran's scared of thunder,' Mum said. 'She and Sophie practically hide under the bed!' She laughed.

'That was years ago when I was little,' I said crossly. I wasn't going to admit that I always think I'll be struck by lightning.

Mum was wearing tiny white shorts and a top which made her look very slim and brown. 'Maybe we'd have done better wearing wellies and macs!' she joked as she put a cake tin in the boat. As the birthday cake was burned, I guessed it was a shop cake out of the freezer.

'Wellies are for wallies!' Jez said and a wheezy giggle escaped from him like a hiss of steam from a kettle. He seemed to be in a weird mood – almost as if he'd had some wine from the bottle Matthew was carrying.

'Who's going to row?' Matthew asked.

'Well, Jez had better have a rest. Fran likes rowing,' Mum said tactlessly. 'I don't know one end of an oar from another.' I didn't want to show up Jez so I said I

71

was useless at rowing, which wasn't true, of course.

Mum sat in the prow of the boat and Jez and I faced Matthew. 'I'll get a new mooring rope when we're next in the town. This one's a bit frayed,' he said as he cast off and rowed downstream.

The boat hadn't been cleaned out for ages and among dead leaves and twigs I saw something red and picked it up. It was a small piece of a red rubber bottle; the top and a bit of one side with a hole in it. Robin's 'holey bottle'! If I'd seen it the other day, I'd have dismissed it as rubbish.

Jez noticed me scrabbling at my feet. 'What's that?' he asked.

'Nothing.' I crammed it into the pocket of the new jeans. When had Robin lost it? Hadn't Fay told me that Gran had never taken them in the boat?

Jez was looking at the swallows swooping low over the river. 'Catching insects. Another sign of rain. I like the way they fly.'

'I always wanted to be a swallow,' I said – then I was afraid he'd laugh but he didn't.

Matthew rowed surprisingly fast for someone of his age and we very soon passed the graveyard wall where I'd first seen Denny. Mum was deliberately looking the other way. 'We'll have to find a field without cows – do you remember how Gran used to tease me about being scared of cows, Fran?'

'Yes.' I took a deep breath. 'Wasn't it about here they found Gran's body?' There was a dire silence and I couldn't look at her. Was I helping her or not?

'Yes, I think so,' she said finally. 'We might find a good picnic place where the river forks at the weir.'

Jez muttered, 'Why did you go reminding your mum about your gran's death? It upsets her.'

'Why not?' I said quietly. 'Why should Gran be forgotten as if she'd done something wrong by dying?'

'It's stupid to have an accident. Can't we be angry with the dead?'

It was a strange thing to say. How could Gran help drowning or his mum help falling from a mountainside?

Matthew rowed down the left-hand channel, away from the thundering weir. 'Let's stop there for the picnic,' I said, pointing at a flat, nettle-free bit of bank where Gran and I had picnicked last summer.

Matthew nosed the boat in and tied it to a tree. When I jumped off the boat, Denny's garland broke and fell into the water. I didn't smile when Matthew made silly jokes about the Little People getting me now I'd lost my protection. I wasn't going to put Fay's silly necklace on after that.

At last we were settled on our rug, under the trees. Matthew suggested a walk but Mum, in her typically Dizzy Izzy high-heeled sandals, made an excuse that it felt thundery and we'd better eat first.

Wasps zoomed down at once and townie Mum kept dancing about, waving at them while Matthew told her they wouldn't sting if she kept still. He opened the bottle of fizzy wine and we were allowed a glass each. They raised their glasses to me and I felt almost happy, for a moment.

Then Mum opened a plastic box and I stared. The cake had shining chocolate icing with wonderful white icing patterns round the words: HAPPY BIRTHDAY FRAN. Mum was busy putting thirteen candles in the holders.

'Brilliant! Thanks!' I said. 'But how...?'

'Matthew made it,' Mum said, smiling fondly at him. 'He offered when he saw mine was burnt.'

'Can't have a birthday without a cake,' he said. 'I started when you went to bed! Helen didn't approve of cakes so I taught myself to bake for occasions. Come on, light the candles.'

I was gobsmacked. Fancy him making the effort for me! 'Thanks,' I said.

We'd got to the cake-lighting and singing 'Happy Birthday' – when I saw Denny, waving from the opposite bank. I waved back but she went out of sight into a clump of trees. Maybe she lived over there.

'Who're you waving at?' Jez asked.

'Just a friend.' Mum reminded me to wish while I blew the candles out. I'd been wishing Mum and I were still on our own. Now, I wasn't so sure. Mum's face literally shone with happiness. And it was the most gorgeous, gooey chocolate cake I'd ever tasted. 'Excellent,' I said. 'Thanks, Matthew.'

He looked pleased. Then he yawned and they both lay back on the rug, holding hands as they stared at the shifting pattern of leaves above them. The next moment they were sound asleep.

Jez smiled at me and poured us out the remainder of the wine and I began to feel relaxed. 'Why don't you talk about your mum's death?' I found myself saying to Jez. 'You've not really told me what happened. It might help.' Then I realised what I'd said. Would he snap at me?

He took off his glasses and wiped them. 'You've got death on the brain, you have,' he said. 'Okay – I'll tell you but it won't help me. She wanted me to climb with her that morning. I was scared of climbing and wouldn't go. Dad stuck up for me and they had a row. Then she went off on her own and – died. So it was sort of my fault, really.'

I was really sorry for him then. 'I think my mum feels guilty too – that she's sort of to blame for Gran's death. She thinks Gran was too old to live on her own. But she's wrong – my gran was strong and healthy.' I tried to think of something to help him. 'Your mum could have fallen when you were climbing with her – you couldn't stop an accident. Wasn't it her fault, anyway? She must have known you didn't like climbing. Maybe she went off so cross that she didn't take enough care.'

'I suppose so.' He crumbled his cake and threw it into the river to a passing pair of ducks. 'I always disappointed her, you know, because I wasn't good at all the outdoor things. I think sometimes even Dad didn't want such energetic holidays but he went to please her.'

He added: 'Don't get me wrong. She was a great mum and I miss her a lot.'

I'd never heard Jez talk so much before. Quite suddenly, my whole picture of Perfect Helen changed into Bossy, Hearty Helen, even Selfish Helen. 'Well, Matthew won't find Mum much of an outdoor type,' I said. 'Her main exercise is dashing in circles and talking her head off!'

Jez smiled and was biting into another piece of cake when a wasp stung him on his lip and almost immediately it began to swell. 'Don't fuss,' he mumbled but I was worried and woke Mum and Matthew, who said he'd got some pills at home which would help. The sky had clouded right over anyway, so we decided to pack up and get back. Matthew began rowing as fast as he could against the current.

Mum looked anxious and dipped a wet teacloth into the river. 'Hold it against the swelling,' she said. Jez did as he was told but his puffed-up lip looked really gross – the swelling seemed to be spreading. He began to wheeze and use his inhaler.

The sky had darkened even more and the air was thick and heavy. Thunder rumbled distantly. People could die of wasp stings. Fay said the Green Woman only did good magic but...

We were just passing the end of Fay's garden when I saw Sophie, swimming towards us, carrying something in her mouth. I yelled at her and then we heard the familiar sound of Robin's screams from the riverbank.

Sophie was near the boat now, only a yard away, a lump of wood in her mouth. Water gushed through holes in the wood... It was Fay's Green Woman! She'd go spare! I stood up in the boat – a thing Gran had always told me not to do, and leaned over. 'Give it to me!' I shouted, reaching out my hand and snatching at the lump of driftwood. Then I was falling, Matthew was shouting and the sky split apart with a crash.

The thunder scared me and I fell in with a great splash, dropping the lump of wood. I rubbed water out of my eyes and saw the Green Woman's head swirling helplessly down river.

Chapter 9

I am sitting in the kitchen, wet through, scared of the thunder and worrying about Jez. Matthew is driving him to the hospital as Jez's face has swollen so much he's finding it hard to breathe. Mum has Robin on her knee. We've already seen the open stable door and the empty box the little boy has stood on to open it.

'It must have been hard for him to undo the hook on the door,' Mum says. 'Thank goodness he didn't fall in the river. I can't understand how he got away without his parents or Fay noticing. I've just phoned – his father's coming over.'

Precious Robin, left on his own – it didn't make sense! He must have trotted into the barn, taken the Green Woman's head, then brought it round to our garden. Then he'd let the dogs out of the stable and Sophie, who so loved carrying things, grabbed the lump of driftwood and plunged into the river – maybe she'd seen our boat coming.

Robin is hiding his face in Mum's lap as the lightning flashes into the room. She is trying to soothe him when there's a bang on the front door.

Mr Gooding bursts in, as loud and angry as the thunder. He says he's been working at his computer while his wife had a rest. 'Fay says she was watching TV with Robin – the idiot girl got bored and went up to her room for a while. When she came down, the storm had started and he'd gone. Then you rang. I'm taking her pocket-money away for a month and as for you, young man...' He bends threateningly over Robin, who clings to Mum and screams.

'You are frightening him,' she says to Mr Gooding and I can tell from the way she spaces her words out that she's getting really angry. 'He's only three. Fay is too young to be a baby-sitter. You should have checked on him.'

Mr Gooding explodes with fury and there's a mega row with my poor mum trying to stand up to him and calm Robin who screams so loudly every time his father tries to grab him that Mum tells him to go. 'I'll dry his clothes and bring him back after the storm,' she says firmly. To my surprise, Mr Gooding slams out, and I just catch a very rude swear-word.

Mum is really worked up by now. 'People like that shouldn't have children or even get married! She ought to leave him!' Then she notices I am still wet and sends me off to change.

As I go upstairs I am more than ever sure that Mr Gooding somehow caused Gran's death. When I'm taking off my wet jeans I find Robin's 'holey bottle' in the pocket and I wonder if this is my chance to ask him when Gran took them out in the boat. I run downstairs and wave it at him.

His tearful face lights up. 'Holey, holey!' he shouts, grabbing the piece of dirty rubber. Balling the rubber top and screw in his fist he sucks his thumb wildly.

'What's that?' Mum asks. 'Did he drop it?'

'Yes, in the boat.' It was too complicated to explain to her. Why had Fay lied and said they'd never been in the boat with Gran? 'Robin – did you go in the boat with Granny Lee?'

'Nasty boat! Robin all alone!' he yells. 'Granny Lee leaves Robin all alone!' And it sets him off crying again.

'Look what you've done, Fran! And he was just calming down,' Mum says. 'And I'm sure Gran never let him get in the boat on his own. He's upset and muddled.'

I am just puzzling over Robin's words when Mrs Gooding and Fay come to the door. Fay's mum is peering out of the hood of her raincoat like a scared little rabbit from its burrow. 'It's all my fault,' she says and rushes in, swooping on Robin. Then she jabbers to Mum all about her husband being so angry and she blames herself.

Fay grabs my arm. 'He's taken my Green Woman,' she whispers. 'After Dad slammed into me I ran out to look.'

I tell her that her Green Woman is swirling down the river. All the colour goes out of her face. 'She can't protect me any more,' she moans.

'Did she ever?' I ask. While Mum is talking quietly to Mrs Gooding I tell Fay quickly about the wasp sting.

'She only did good spells…' Fay begins and then Mrs Gooding is thanking Mum and hurrying the children home to face the Ogre.

Mum tries to cheer me up by making coffee and suggesting we have some more birthday cake. I try to eat but for once, I'm not hungry because I'm worried about Jez. Mum guesses and gives me a hug. 'He'll be fine,' she says yet again. It's just the two of us, like it used to be but I want Matthew to bring Jez safely back.

Mum cradles her mug of coffee in her hands and looks out of the curtainless window as a zigzag of lightning flashes across the sky. It is so dark outside that I can barely see the apple tree. Obediah looks down at the dogs from the top of the kitchen cupboard. Sophie has squashed herself into Bas's basket and he's resting his furrowed muzzle on her back. I wish I could curl up with them.

'You know I'm very happy with Matthew, don't you, Fran?' Mum says suddenly. 'I love him a lot and also he makes me feel secure. I just wish Jez would accept me. I think he likes you, Fran. But it's very early days yet.'

I'm not sure that Jez does like me but I'm glad she's happy. Matthew's certainly not my idea of a dream-hunk but at Mum's age I suppose she couldn't be too choosy. At least he was kind and he certainly could make brilliant chocolate cake. 'He's certainly better than some of the real weeds and dorks you went out with,' I say, and she laughs.

The flickering storm whitens her face as she goes on:

'Your father – he was great fun, Fran, and we had good times together – but now you're older maybe you ought to know that I was very worried about money at times. He never held on to a job. Sometimes he seemed like a boy. But I grew tired of always being the grown-up. That's when he looked after you and I started work at Jeans Unlimited. I couldn't be Dizzy Izzy then. That came later.' She sighs. 'It's right for you to think he was a great dad – he was, in his way – but you've built him up into Superman.'

I feel a kind of shock as if a picture has been broken. I don't know what to say, so there's a silence, interrupted by Matthew and Jez coming back. Jez is pale but the swelling on his lip is going down. Matthew says he's had a special injection.

'We drove right through the storm!' Jez says. 'It was magic!'

Magic! I tell myself off for ever thinking the Green Woman was more than a lump of wood. Jez has just been unlucky lately.

Mum filled her car with jeans ready for work on Monday and we watched a silly film on TV while we ate Matthew's pancakes dripping with golden syrup. Jez fell asleep in his chair, his face pale but peaceful.

The storm had stopped by the time I went to bed but heavy rain pelted against my window. I kept seeing the Green Woman's head floating down the river. Poor Fay – she had so little. What would she do without her magic?

I still didn't see why Fay said they'd not been in the boat. If I could find out just when Robin dropped his piece of bottle – and had it anything to do with Gran's death? Ideas floated into my mind. Supposing Gran took the children out and Mr Gooding was angry. I saw him meeting the boat, then Fay and Robin jumping out and running away – Mr Gooding with his arm raised, Gran having a heart attack and then Mr Gooding pushing the boat into the river to make it look as if she'd fallen out.

But that still left two practical questions. Why would they be out early in the morning and, if dear Gran was already dead, lying in the boat, how did she fall out? I tossed and turned, unable to think of the answer. My story would explain why Fay and Robin denied going in the boat, trying to cover up for their dad. He'd probably threatened them into silence.

At last I went to sleep. I dreamed that Denny was up the apple tree amongst the moon-silvered fruit. She was waving the Green Woman's head at me and it grew enormous, suddenly turning into Jez. He laughed and threw me a silver apple and I felt so happy. Then, suddenly, I was in the river. It was dark and scary and Jez was somewhere nearby, calling for help. When I got to him he turned into Gran, floating in her nightie. I couldn't get hold of her and the wet cloth somehow wound round me, drawing me down . . . My legs were so heavy.

I woke, sweating, with my head under the duvet and both Sophie and Obediah curled heavily on my legs.

The rain had stopped and a thin finger of moonlight came through the curtains. I got up and drew them back. The full moon was silvering the leaves and apples on the tree, just like my dream. The cool air smelled of wet earth and grass. There wasn't the slightest breeze and yet as I watched, there was a movement in the apple tree and I heard the faint plop as an apple fell to the ground. 'Denny!' I called but nobody answered.

It took a long time to go to sleep again and when I came downstairs late next morning, Mum was just going off to work – she said Matthew had already left. 'Don't forget the bookshelves are coming this morning,' she called. 'And could you find the key to the barn? We want to sort it out.'

So Fay would lose her private place. But maybe she'd not want to go there without her Green Woman. I ate some muesli and then went to look for Jez. I found him at last in the old stable, taking the bent rear wheel off his bike. He loosened the last screw and picked the wheel up. 'Taking it to be mended in town – the bus is due now – got to go,' he said and ran off.

I'd been all ready to ask him how he felt now and I'd planned to say he ought to take it easy – and wait for the bookshelves. It wasn't fair – now I had to stay in when I wanted to find Denny and then maybe talk to Mrs Gooding if her husband was safely away at work. I thought Jez hadn't enough money to get the bike mended. Matthew must have given him some, after all.

I was crossly washing up the breakfast things when I

remembered I was seeing Hills the next day. Perhaps I could tell her my ideas about Gran's death: I could trust her and it wouldn't upset her too much. There was no point in getting my mum worked up until I was sure I had the answer to the mystery and we could do something about it.

The dogs heard the van before I did. The man dumped the bookcase in the hall and I fetched the envelope from behind the kitchen clock. There were two twenty-pound notes. I did a double take. Surely there should be eighty pounds, not forty? 'Can't you leave the bookshelves and we'll send the extra?' I asked. The man shook his head. 'Cash on delivery, sorry, love. You try running a second-hand business any other way. I'll come back tomorrow.'

When he'd gone back to his van, a horrible thought came into my mind. One minute Jez hadn't enough money and the next he could pay for his bike repairs. I couldn't believe he'd do it – but there was nobody else. How could he have thought he'd not get found out? Unless... another nasty thought came along – unless he'd wanted Mum and Matthew to think I was the thief!

I decided to lock up the house and ask Denny's advice. I took the camera and the dogs.

I relaxed as soon as I was walking through the trees towards the den and I even took some pictures of the sunlight glittering on the rain-bowed bracken. There was a smell of pine needles and wet leaves. A small deer rushed across the path and the dogs ran after it. I ran along, calling them and I was just wondering which way they'd gone when Denny walked towards me, a dog on either side. As she waved, she was spot-lit by a shaft of sunlight and I just had to take another picture.

'Hope the photo comes out,' she said. 'Let's go to my den.' As I followed her, I thanked her for the berry necklace. 'It was all I could give you. It was to protect you against fear. Plant seeds of fear and they grow.'

The den was puddled with water from the over-flowing river, so we sat on the willow trunk, now only just above the swollen water. I stared at the branches and twigs whirling downstream and thought it would be dangerous to swim now.

I told her I was sure Mr Gooding was involved in Gran's death. Then I described what had happened after I saw Denny on my birthday and, last of all, the puzzle of the missing money and my worry that Jez had taken it.

She listened in silence, peeling bark off an elder twig, leaving the black berries.

'Well, what should I do?' I asked at the end.

She was silent a moment, watching a moorhen as it chuntered into a clump of reeds. Then she said: 'Let's start with the money. Did Fay know it was there?'

I tried to remember. 'She might've – she was there when they put it behind the clock – but why should she take it? The Goodings don't seem short of money.'

'Maybe she's jealous – she doesn't want to share you with Jez. Poor Fay – she's got nobody but a bullying father and a nervous mum.' She threw the peeled twig into the fast-flowing river. It was dashed this way and that by the current before it disappeared downstream.

'I suppose it could have been Fay. But what should I do about it? And how can I get Mr Gooding to confess? No good just asking him because he'd say no and probably get really mad at me.'

She rubbed some mud off her knees. Fay was right in a way, Denny did get herself really mucky from working on a farm and scrambling around the river. She spoke slowly: 'I reckon someone has to get Mrs Gooding to tell on her husband, to be prepared to give him away. He *has* to be stopped. He's at the bottom of all the trouble.'

She bent down and kissed Sophie's woolly head and Bas pushed up, licking her hand. 'I have to go now.' She sighed. 'I'd like to stay with you but I'm needed at home. We've started harvesting.' She touched my arm. 'You're older than me. You need to decide things for yourself now you're a teenager. I reckon that's the hard bit about growing up.' She grinned. 'I don't want to grow up, myself.' Then she looked really serious, almost sad. 'Fran – I can't help you any more. I wish I could, I really do.'

She climbed up and balanced on the willow above the foaming river and her whole body glowed with dancing life, like moving motes of dust in a shaft of sunshine.

'Why do you always have to rush off?' I felt cross with her for leaving me alone with my problems.

She turned round mid-stream, her dirty bare feet gripping the willow-bark. 'I told you – I'm needed back home. We'll always be best friends, Fran.' She jumped off on the opposite bank and waved before plunging through a gap in the undergrowth.

I felt as if a light had gone out. I told myself I'd see her again soon but she'd left a lonely space.

When I got back, Jez was sitting on the doorstep, looking cross. 'I need a key,' he complained as we went inside.

'At least I stayed in for the bookshelves and that was a waste of time. Someone's nicked half the money. You knew where it was, didn't you?' Whatever Denny hinted about Fay, I thought Jez could have just 'borrowed' the money, meaning to put it back.

He gave me a dirty look. 'What are you going on about?'

'You were there, in the kitchen when Mum left the money behind the clock for the bookshelves. Didn't you hear her?'

He freaked out at once. 'You saying I took it?'

'I just wondered if you might have borrowed it for your bike repairs.'

'I don't pinch money and I'm not stupid!' he shouted. 'They'd soon find out if I had. And what about *you*?'

'Well, I didn't.' I tried to keep cool. 'And I don't need the money like you do. How did you get enough to have your wheel repaired?'

'It's not done yet – I'll collect it tomorrow and it's my business how I pay.'

It seemed very likely he'd stolen the money but I didn't want him to get into trouble. 'If you tell them straight off, maybe they won't be so angry.'

'Get lost!' and he slammed the door as he went out again.

Of course, I wasn't sure then. Perhaps he hadn't done it. I told myself I'd feel angry if I'd been falsely accused of stealing. As I made myself a sandwich I thought of Denny's hints about Fay and I wished I'd not said anything to Jez.

The front doorbell rang. As if my thoughts had brought her, Fay stood on the step, crying. 'What's the matter?' I asked.

'Everything.' She followed me in, sniffing. 'And Mum's worse after yesterday. Robin's got a cold and Mum behaves as if he's dying. My dad – he's mega-angry and blames me. He . . . ' She stopped. 'Where's Jez?'

'In the garden. He's angry with me because some money left in the kitchen went missing and I blamed him.'

'What money?' she asked, too innocently.

'You were there – you must've seen Mum put it behind the clock. Eighty pounds and now forty is missing. Did you take it?'

Her face didn't change. 'What would I want money for?' she said. 'I've got loads of clothes and tapes and everything. I expect your stepbrother took it. I just came to talk.' Her voice was low and shaky. 'It's awful at home with Mum fussing over Robin as if he's got the plague. The doctor's been already and it's only a cold.' Her nose was running. 'Got a tissue?' she asked plaintively.

I couldn't help feeling sorry for her. 'All right. We'll go upstairs in case Jez comes in.' I found the tissues and Fay slumped on my bed, blowing her nose. The telephone rang downstairs. It was Hills, asking after Jez. 'You won't forget to come and see me tomorrow?' she said when I'd told her he was better. I promised I would. There was a lot to tell her.

When I went back, Fay wasn't in my room. I found her reading something on Jez's computer screen. 'Why're you nosing about in here?' I asked angrily.

She looked up calmly. 'Read this. He must've taken the money.'

It was part of Jez's diary, dated the day before. He must have forgotten to close down.

Didn't want to go on Fran's birthday picnic but we got a bit friendly over the wine and I told her about Mum's death. Got stung by a wasp and had to go to hospital – a bit scary but brilliant coming back through the storm. Dad won't give me money for bike repairs – it's not fair. I'll use the money I stealed to have it done. Don't care what he says after.

'See!' Fay said triumphantly. 'I didn't take it! Say sorry!'

'Okay – sorry,' I said slowly. I couldn't understand why I felt sad that Jez was a thief, after all. He was silly leaving his computer diary on. Then I remembered my important question. 'When did Robin lose that bottle thing of his?' When she didn't answer I asked her again, louder.

90

'Don't shout!' she said crossly. 'How should I remember? Weeks ago.' She was looking out of the window. 'I can see Jez. He might come inside. We'd better get out of his room.'

She wasn't going to get away from me. I followed her to the landing and gripped her arm. 'Did Robin lose his "holey bottle" the day Gran died? I found it in the boat and you said Gran never took you out in it.'

'Stop it! You're hurting! We didn't go in the boat with her!' She twisted free and ran downstairs and I heard the front door slam.

I went down to the kitchen. Sophie came up and nudged me and I realised I'd forgotten to feed the dogs and Jez certainly hadn't remembered. As I filled their bowls I knew I wanted to cover up for him, I wasn't sure why. I ran upstairs. The computer was a bit different from the one at school but I managed to close the file, leaving the screen-saver on.

Then I couldn't think what to do. I lay on my bed with Sophie curled at my feet and listened to the CD Jez had given me. My mind kept going in circles. Jez would be back soon and I didn't know what to say to him. But I must have dozed because Sophie woke me, running to the door and joining in Bas's deeper barking.

Matthew was downstairs, back from work.

I ran downstairs and almost immediately he asked if the bookshelves had arrived. My heart beat fast. 'The man came but there wasn't enough money so he's coming back.' I was stammering and my face felt hot. I didn't want Jez to get into trouble.

He stared. 'What do you mean?'

I'd put the envelope behind the clock again. He took it down and stared at the notes. 'Forty pounds missing! Someone must have taken it. Did anyone come into the kitchen, earlier? Maybe someone broke in and took it while we were out on the picnic – but everything was locked.'

'Maybe,' I said miserably.

'I'd rather know the truth if either of you borrowed the money,' Matthew said slowly. 'I can't stand lies. Did you take it, Fran?' I shook my head. 'Jez needed money for his bike,' he said, almost to himself, and he went upstairs.

Bas looked up at me soulfully as if he understood and I stroked those long, drooping ears, then Sophie's curly head nudged me for attention. There were angry voices upstairs and Matthew came back alone. He looked at me as if he wanted to say something but stopped himself.

'Fay was alone in the kitchen for a while,' I said quickly. 'It could have been her.'

His face was set and he didn't answer. Obviously he was sure Jez had taken the money. 'I'm going to paint the kitchen ceiling, Fran. I think there's a stepladder in the shed. And have you found the barn door key?'

Jez didn't appear and I helped Matthew put things away and cover surfaces with old sheets. When Matthew began painting, I slipped upstairs and opened Jez's door. He was lying on his bed, pretending to read. When he looked up I saw his eyelids were red and swollen. 'Go away!' he shouted. 'So you've pinned the blame on me – are you satisfied? Do you think I'd be such a dork – take the money when they'd find out?'

'I never said anything! But you wrote you'd taken it in your computer diary!'

'Sneaking into my room!' He jumped up as if he might hit me and went to his computer. When he'd opened the file he stared at the words on the screen. Then he turned round, his face twisted with anger. 'You use a computer at school, don't you? I never wrote that sentence – you must have done! But you're not too bright, are you? I'd never put "stealed" instead of "stole"! And if I'd taken the money I'd not have been such a wally as to write about it. I suppose it was your idea of a joke. Get out!'

So I did, feeling hurt that he thought I'd added to his computer diary – and stolen the money for a joke! Looking back, I should have stayed and told him it must have been Fay – but he was in no mood to listen.

I slipped out of the house while Matthew was up the stepladder in the kitchen. I had to get Fay to admit she was a thief. Mrs Gooding took ages to answer the door. 'Is Fay there?' I asked.

'Don't talk loudly. I've just got my Robin to sleep,' she whispered. 'No – she's gone off somewhere. She doesn't care about her little brother being so poorly.'

Where was Fay? Had she run off because she was guilty?

As I walked in our front door, there was a crash and a shout from the kitchen. I found Matthew on the floor with the broken stepladder on top of him. There was paint all over the floor.

'What's happened? I heard a noise.' Jez looked horrified at the scene. We moved the ladder with its broken top off Matthew. He got up stiffly, saying he was all right, just bruised.

'I'd forgotten – Gran said she needed a new stepladder,' I said, feeling guilty.

'Sure you're okay, Dad?' Jez asked.

'Yes,' Matthew snapped. 'And you get back to your room.'

'I tell you, I didn't take your rotten money!' Jez rushed upstairs and slammed his door. Bas, sensing something was wrong, lumbered after him.

I had to find Fay and prove Jez was innocent. In his present mood, he could do anything. I suppose she could be in the woods but the most likely place was the barn. Well, Matthew wanted the key, anyway. I looked through all the keys I could find and tried the two most likely on the barn door. One fitted and I walked in.

Something had happened to the pictures. They were covered in black scribble. The candles were lit again on either side of the bare altar. In front of it, Fay was curled up like a baby with Obediah, surrounded by a huge ring of dolls, their eyes glittering in the candlelight. It was a scary, awesome sight. 'Fay,' I said but she didn't move. Obediah looked up at me as if to say, 'Keep away.'

I pushed between an overdressed Spanish doll and a golden-haired baby doll, knocking them over. 'Sorry,' I said – Oh, now I was going bananas too!

I touched her on the shoulder. 'You all right?'

'No,' she said in a muffled voice, choked with sobs. 'The Green Woman's gone. I'm alone now.'

'Stop feeling sorry for yourself and tell me the truth. Jez is in trouble over the money. Can you type on a computer keyboard?'

'Yes. My dad's got one.'

'You altered his diary, didn't you?'

She sat up then. 'He'd left his screen on. It was my chance. I was getting rid of him for you, wasn't I? I thought if he got into trouble about the money they'd make him board at school after all.'

'So you did steal it?' I shouted, so loudly Obediah shot off.

'Yes I did!' The words came out in tearful jerks. 'But I've not spent it. I'd have given it back after they sent him away – I'd have slipped it through the door.'

'Pull the other one!'

'I would, I would!' she shouted. Then she curled up again on the floor, crying and sucking her thumb. I had to tell Matthew! I ran out of the barn and found him asleep in front of the TV. 'Wake up! Fay's confessed she stole the money!' I shouted.

'What?' Matthew sat up, looking completely gobsmacked as I told him what had happened.

'I think she sort of thought I wanted Jez to board at

school – and if you got mad at him you might send him away.'

Matthew got up and hobbled across the room. 'I'd better apologise to Jez.' He called him but Jez didn't answer so I offered to go as Matthew's leg was obviously painful.

Jez's bedroom is empty and the computer is humming to itself. I look at the screen – the diary has gone and the cursor is blinking at words written in capitals:

I DIDN'T DO IT DAD!!
I'M GOING OUT IN THE BOAT TO GET AWAY
FROM YOU ALL.

'He's gone in the boat!' I call to Matthew as I run out of the back door. I race down the garden and in the gathering dusk I see Jez rowing awkwardly downstream, Bas sitting beside him. Sophie is dancing up and down the bank, barking. Matthew calls from the lighted doorway. 'Get help!' I shout. 'He doesn't know about the current by the weir! It'll be too strong for him.' I have to go after Jez. He isn't strong and hasn't done any rowing. The swollen river is running fast and he'll not have strength to row alone against the pull of the weir.

When I get to the bank, I just catch a glimpse of Jez and Bas before the storm-swollen water has whirled them out of sight. Jez doesn't know how to use the oars properly and he hasn't a clue how to keep the boat straight.

'Jez!' I call, but he can't hear – the rushing water drowns my voice. Is he running away or just mad at everyone? I think of the fast current and wonder if Matthew and I could get ahead of him by car? But Matthew's hurt his leg and I'm not sure he can drive. It would be much quicker to swim after the boat.

Luckily I'm wearing shorts so I kick my sandals off and plunge in. The storm water feels icy. There's a splash behind me and then Sophie nudges my shoulder and I know she is swimming beside me. The current is strong and takes me down river swiftly. A stick hits my back and my face is scratched on swirling twigs and leaves.

I'm cold... and I feel the current sweeping me along. Will I catch him up in time? He doesn't know the river and its dangers. He's on the wrong side, where the fast water drags boats towards the weir. We used to keep well into the bank and even then, when the river was full after a storm, like this, Gran and I had to paddle fast, an oar each, to keep straight.

Here's the graveyard wall already. I'm being pulled to the wrong side. How long to the weir? I've swum a mile in the school pool but not this far in the river. I can hear Sophie panting behind me. 'Get back!' I call to her but she takes no notice.

Oh, Jez, I haven't had time to know you yet! You can't drown! I see again the head of the Green Woman bobbing away down the river. It's all my fault, not realising he was so unhappy and making Fay think I wanted him to go away...

I swallow some river water as I look ahead. I can just see the boat in the dusky light. It's slewing round towards the opening to the weir! I change to my fastest crawl and see that Jez knows he's in danger – he's pushing Bas into the water and following him. The empty boat is already yards ahead, bobbing towards the weir. Weedy Jez will never be able to swim in this strong current.

'Jez!' I call, getting a mouthful of river water, then, somehow I'm there and Sophie ploughs towards the bank with Bas following. Suddenly Jez isn't swimming any more and I'm on my back, my hands under his armpits, bringing him in as I've learned in life-saving class, but this is for real and the current is pushing us towards the weir. Oh, Gran, am I drowning?

Then Denny is there, beside me, holding me up so I can pull Jez to the bank.

The dogs shook themselves all over me as I tried to put Jez in the recovery position but he struggled with me, coughing. Then he was sick. 'I'm all right,' he said slowly.

'He's okay, Denny!' I shouted but she'd gone – perhaps for help? Then I saw Mum, running towards us.

She was panting like she'd done a marathon as she threw her arms round me: 'I thought you'd both drown!' And then she leant over Jez, who was wheezing and coughing.

'I'm all right,' he managed to say.

She held him as he staggered to his feet. 'Matthew's coming. He can't walk fast. We've left the car by the church,' she gabbled. 'I'd just got in from work and I found Matthew trying to run down the back lawn to the river with some idea of swimming after you. He told me what had happened – he'd remembered the weir so he was crazy with worry. I thought we'd catch you up in the car if we hurried as the road runs parallel to the river.'

Matthew hobbled up. He rushed to Jez, hugging him as if he'd come back from the dead – which I guess he nearly had!

Jez managed to get up and walk, with his father's arm round him. I tried to explain to Matthew what had happened as we went back to the car. 'You were brave, Fran,' he said. 'Jez might have drowned, otherwise.'

I was just going to tell them about Denny helping when we came to the car and bundled inside, the wet dogs going into the boot-space. I sat next to Mum, who was driving, Matthew had his arm round Jez at the back. As we started off I heard him say, 'You shouldn't have run away, Jez. I was coming to apologise – apparently Fay took the money.'

'Fay – that figures,' Jez said hoarsely. 'But I wasn't running away. I just wanted to . . . scare you. I was angry because you thought I was a thief. And I wanted to try to row the boat. But I made a mess of that, didn't I?'

It was Mum who asked: 'Why did Fay take the money?'

She never got an answer because as we drove round

the corner we saw smoke, pale against the gathering darkness: small flames shot up, sending sparks like fireworks.

'Our barn!' Mum cried out. 'It's on fire!'

Chapter 10

'Fay – she's probably in there!' I yelled as we parked the car outside Folly Farm.

Mum hurried Jez into our house, saying she'd ring the Fire Service.

I ran to the barn door, quite forgetting we hadn't collected the key, Matthew hobbling after me. Sneaky little orange-red flames spurted out of the roof and the thick smoke was pouring under the door. 'Fay!' I shouted, uselessly. I rushed back, into the road and through the Goodings' garden. I could hear Matthew shouting after me but I ran under the willow. This wall of the barn was still intact but when I opened the little door smoke poured out. I reeled back, coughing. Then Denny was there, beside me. 'Smoke rises, Fran – crawl on all fours,' she said in a calm voice. I obeyed. As I went into the barn I remember thinking in a muddled way that I was so wet I'd not get burned. Somewhere behind me Matthew was calling out and I thought I heard Mrs Gooding screaming Fay's name.

Small flames shot up ahead and lit up a dark shape coming towards me. Fay's white face was lit up by the blaze. I hung on to her and someone was pulling me backwards – out of the barn so I could breathe. 'Fran!'

Matthew was shouting and Mrs Gooding was screaming. It was only then that I saw Fay was clutching Obediah.

'Is he dead?' she spluttered. 'I went to save him.'

'I told her not to go,' Mrs Gooding said in a shaky voice.

Suddenly there was a kind of explosion and a huge flame leaped up into the sky. 'Gran kept petrol for the mower in there,' I stuttered as Matthew urged us all away.

Where was Denny? Then in the strange light of the fire I saw her dark, stocky shape ahead of us, waving as she ran down the Goodings' lawn to the river.

We heard a faint screaming from the house. 'Robin! I had to lock him in!' cried Mrs Gooding and she ran to him.

'Obediah!' Fay kept crying. The limp bundle in her arms suddenly stiffened into life and I heard a feeble meow.

Fay and I clutched each other hysterically. 'He's alive! You saved him!' I said between bouts of coughing.

After that, it was all confusion. Mum insisted on the Goodings coming back to Folly Farm. She and Matthew took an exhausted Jez up to bed. Then the fire engine came and Matthew went outside.

Fay, sitting white-faced in the kitchen, trying to drink tea, burst into tears. 'I must have left a candle burning. And somehow it fell over. I'm sorry.'

'You've been playing in their barn,' Mrs Gooding repeated dully and now I saw she had a black eye. 'I didn't know. I suppose she went to hide from her father.' Mrs Gooding clasped Robin to her.

Fay was still holding Obediah, who was clutching at her, claws out but half-conscious, his eyes yellow slits. Suddenly he woke and jumped off her lap. Bas, scared by the noise of the fire, had retreated to his basket but Sophie immediately began to lick the cat's face. 'Look, he's all right!' Fay said delightedly as Obediah, remembering his dignity, moved slowly away from Sophie and went to climb the back stairs to his favourite sleeping place, my bed.

'You go up and change, Fran,' Mum said, throwing me a towel. I was shaking from cold and fear. Through the back window I saw people moving against the smoke and the house lights lit up the powerful jets of water but the flames had died down.

'Why are you all wet?' Fay asked me.

'Jez nearly drowned,' I said angrily. 'It's all your fault, taking the money and making him take the blame. That's why he took the boat out.' My legs were weak from shock and swimming and I slumped into a chair.

'I didn't spend it!' she said again. 'And I did it for you, Fran, so he'd get into trouble and be sent away to school. But your gran's death...that was sort of my fault.' She couldn't finish. Tears poured down her dirty face.

I stood up shakily with some confused idea of making

them all listen. 'It wasn't Fay's fault, it was her father who scared Gran to death. Fay's covering up for him because she's scared of him. Because he hits her.'

'What do you mean?' Mrs Gooding's voice was high and almost hysterical. 'He went off early that morning – about six. He had to drive to Wales. It's true, he's violent and hits us all but he never touched your granny. If I'd thought it was him, I'd have told the police and got him out of the way.' She began to cry and Mum went over to her.

I sat down again, suddenly dizzy. I had been so sure it was Mr Gooding. Then I remembered. 'Fay – you said you hadn't been in the boat but you had. I found Robin's holey bottle there. Why did you lie?'

She wiped her hand over her face, streaking down tears and dirt. 'I didn't lie. I didn't go in the boat. I'll explain only don't tell my dad or he'll kill me,' she whispered. 'You see, your gran came to baby-sit when Mum and Dad went out, that night before she died. She said if Mum agreed she'd take us out in the boat next day. I wanted to go alone with her, not always with Robin tagging along but Robin cried and she said he'd have to come too. She'd put him to bed and was sort of dozing in front of the telly so I slipped out to the barn. Robin must've got up and came out after me, so I gave him a tiny smack and told him to go back to bed.' She looked at her mother. 'The barn was my place, not his. And it was somewhere Dad couldn't come.'

'Oh, Fay!' said Mrs Gooding. 'How could you smack

our little baby?' She clutched Robin so hard she woke him up and he began to whimper quietly.

Fay took no notice. 'Your gran heard the crying and ran out. She found the little door behind the willow. When she was inside, Robin put on an act and yelled, saying I'd smacked him. So she got mad at me. Then she saw my paintings and the . . . ' She stopped. I guessed she wasn't going to talk about the Green Woman. 'She told me how worried she was about us all. I tried to make her promise not to tell Them that Dad hit us all because we could get sent away – to a Home – but she said she had to think it over.'

Mrs Gooding looked totally shocked. 'I never knew you went there, Fay dear. It's not our barn. Your dad would be ever so angry . . . ' Then she added so quietly that I think only I heard: 'But he won't know. He's gone.' What did she mean? But Fay gabbled on as if she couldn't stop.

'Your gran promised she'd not say anything about me playing in the barn. She knew I needed a special place. Robin was still making a fuss, so she said she'd take him out in the boat next day if Mum agreed, on his own. She said I had to learn to treat him properly or I could end up like Dad. I didn't see why she should take Robin in the boat and not me. I wanted to be with her.' She stopped to wipe her face again.

'So what happened?' Mum asked tensely.

'Robin and I went to bed but I heard Mum and Dad come back. I heard Dad talking to your gran and the front door opened and shut. I suppose he was taking your gran home. Then he was back and began to row with Mum. It sounded as if he hit her because she sort of gasped.'

Mrs Gooding was ghost-white and her voice quavered as she spoke: 'He accused me of being disloyal, of telling Mrs Lee he'd hit us. I never did but I should have.'

I still didn't understand. 'What happened about the boat?' I asked. 'How did Gran die? Your dad could have gone round and bullied her into a heart attack early next morning.'

'He didn't because I saw her alive next day.' Fay spoke so fast and disjointedly it was hard to hear her. 'I didn't sleep for ages because of Dad hitting Mum, then I woke up when he drove off – around six.' She looked at them pleadingly. 'It was sort of like hating him had made me mad with everyone, specially Robin. I just wanted your gran on her own. So I decided to get rid of the boat so Robin couldn't go out in it. I got dressed and went through our gate and along the riverbank to your garden. I didn't want to hurt anyone!' She was sobbing now. 'I thought I'd just undo the rope from that ring – so the boat would float away. Then they couldn't go out in it. I'd only half undone it when I saw your gran looking out of her bedroom window, so I ran back and hid in the barn. I loved your gran. I didn't want her to die!' Then she started sobbing again, her head on the table. Her mother put Robin down and went to hug her.

Mum tried to speak but her voice was sort of strangled.

Suddenly I saw the whole scene, like on a video. 'Robin woke up,' I said. 'He came out to the barn and saw you. Maybe you slapped him again – anyway, he ran down the garden and through the gate – that you'd left open – calling Gran. He didn't wait for her but got into the boat ready for his trip. You'd loosened the rope – so the boat floated off with Robin inside. That's when he dropped his holey bottle. Gran saw it all from the window – rushed down the garden. She must've decided to swim to the boat...' I found my voice was wobbling. 'And I guess Robin somehow fell in – but she fished him out and pushed him up the bank. But it was too much for her heart. I suppose she fell back into the water.' My voice had gone hoarse and I had to stop a moment. 'Afterwards, the current carried her body downstream.' I couldn't go on and Mum was crying.

I found I was shouting: 'Then I suppose Robin rushed back, dripping wet and yelling and because he doesn't talk very well you didn't understand that Gran was in the river?'

'Yes, yes! If only I'd known...' Fay couldn't go on. 'I thought he'd fallen in or something.'

Robin was listening to us. 'Granny Lee go away. Come back to see Robin.' It was the first time I'd heard him say so much.

'That's what he said, more or less. I didn't understand...' her voice trailed off.

'Why didn't you tell me, Fay darling?' Mrs Gooding spoke almost in a whisper.

'Because you were doped with your pills after your bad night, remember, Mum?' Fay said.

'Yes. It was a terrible night. Your father drank too much. But you could have woken me up. Poor Robin! Nearly drowning...like...'

'Robin not to tell about getting wet. Fay gave me sweeties,' Robin said. He climbed on a chair to look out of the window. 'Firemen!' he said happily.

'I didn't want you to worry, Mum,' Fay said. 'Not with Dad getting worse. You couldn't take any more. It was only after they found...Fran's granny in the river that I worked out what might have happened.' She looked at my mum. 'I've felt awful ever since. Sort of like I murdered her.' Her head went down on the table again and her crying went all shuddery, like a little kid's.

Mum took a deep breath. She got up and put her hand on Fay's shoulder. 'It was still an accident. It was wrong to undo that mooring rope but you mustn't feel guilty, Fay. After all, my mother often swam in the river – just this time her heart gave out. It was too cold for her.' Of course she was being kind because it wasn't true. We knew Gran was used to swimming in the river, even in spring, if it was warm. It had been her efforts to rescue Robin that had killed her.

At that moment Matthew hobbled in, smelling of bonfires. 'They've got it under control now but the inside's gutted.' He looked round the room. 'Don't worry – it was only an old barn and the stone walls are standing. But thank goodness the fire didn't spread.'

'Fay's been telling us what she knows about Gran's death,' Mum was saying. 'She thinks it was an accident – Robin got in the boat and it drifted off, then Gran rescued him but the cold water was too much for her heart.'

Matthew looked at Fay and Mrs Gooding's arms tightened round her protectively. 'Why didn't you tell the police?' he asked.

'It wouldn't bring her back. And my dad would have beaten us,' Fay said, sobbing.

Gran said you'd got to put yourself in other people's shoes. I'd laughed at the expression but she said you had to imagine how they felt. I got into Fay's shoes and knew how guilty and sad she had been all this time. It wasn't a good feeling. Thankfully, I stepped back into my own shoes and gave her a box of tissues.

'Gran wouldn't have wanted you to cry like this,' I said. 'You said she wanted to help you.'

'I wanted to be your friend,' Fay said. 'Now you'll hate me.'

I thought about it. 'I won't,' I said.

Mum smiled at her. 'You can come over here any time. That is, if your parents are happy about it.'

Mrs Gooding hugged Fay harder. She looked at Mum, almost with triumph. 'My husband's gone. He hit Fay again when he came in. That's why she went to the barn. I told him you'd seen the bruises and you'd very likely report him. So I said I'd tell the police and the Welfare people about him hitting us and I'd got a witness. So – after he'd given me this – ' She fingered the black eye. 'He packed a suitcase and went – said he'd go to his girlfriend. I pity her, I do really.' Her voice wobbled into silence.

'You were very brave,' Mum told her.

'He deserves to be punished!' Matthew said angrily. 'I wish we'd reported him.'

Fay sat up straight. 'Dad's really gone? That's amazing! But supposing he comes back?'

'We'll be here to fetch the police,' Matthew said. 'We should have helped you earlier.'

Fay picked up Robin, who was trying to dry Sophie with a tea towel. 'Our horrible dad's gone, Robin! We're free!'

'Horrible Dad!' Robin repeated. 'Gone away!' and he began to laugh, Fay joining in.

'If you need any help...' Mum said. 'Shopping...'

'Gardening,' said Matthew.

Mrs Gooding smiled through her tears. 'You are so kind. I won't need my pills now he's gone so I shall do more. But I am worried about Fay.'

Mum smiled at her. 'You'll be all right, won't you, Fay? This will all fade, gradually, as you start a new life. You might need to talk to someone about it all.'

'Yes. Talking helps,' Matthew said thoughtfully. 'School soon and maybe you'd like to come out with us at weekends sometimes.'

I was amazed. I thought he'd have hated Fay, for

making Jez suffer and for all her lies – to say nothing of the fire in the barn. He was kind, I knew that already. Well, if he and Mum were prepared to try to untangle Fay from her memories of beatings and from her magic, I'd help too. She would never become a best friend, like Denny, but I guess we'd rub along together.

When the Goodings had gone Matthew made scrambled eggs while I had a hot bath. Jez ate his in bed and went to sleep again. I dried the dogs and fed them. Then the room seemed to be going round me and there was a roaring in my ears.

I opened my eyes and found I was in bed. Matthew and Mum were standing over me, looking anxious. 'You fainted,' Mum said.

'How did I get upstairs?'

'I won't say you were light as a feather...' Matthew was smiling down at me.

'You carried me?' My face was hot.

'Why not? At least my bad leg didn't give way. And I like carrying heroines.'

'You'll make her swollen-headed,' Mum joked. 'But we're very proud of you, Fran, for rescuing Jez and then Fay.'

I tried to say something but my eyelids were so heavy. I knew there was something I still hadn't told them. 'I didn't do it on my own; Denny helped me,' I muttered and zonked out.

Chapter 11

When I woke next morning the room was full of sunshine. It must be late. Yesterday seemed like one of my nightmares.

When I went downstairs, Jez was eating his muesli and Matthew was making toast. 'Hi, Fran,' he said. 'Your mum's gone to work and I'm taking a day off to rest my leg – but it already feels better. I can drive our car as it's automatic. I shall go to town with Jez to fetch his bike wheel. Your mum wanted me to take him to the doctor but he seems remarkably recovered. How do you feel?'

'Fine.' While Matthew was letting the dogs out I asked Jez where he got the money for the bike repairs. 'I thought you hadn't got any money.'

'Post office book – mine, from my dad's desk.' Matthew was back now and Jez looked at him rather defiantly. 'That money I'm never supposed to spend.'

Matthew smiled and rested his hand lightly on Jez's shoulder. 'I'm very sorry I didn't believe you.' Then he went out to have another look at the remains of the barn.

'Thanks for fishing me out of the river, Fran.' Jez looked embarrassed. 'I suppose you think I'm a real dork. I was so mad at Dad not believing me about the money. And I was sick of seeming so weedy. So I thought I'd just show everyone and row down river. I wanted to worry Dad.' He grinned. 'I succeeded a bit too well!'

I was starving so I poured out some cereal for myself and thought hard as I stirred in the milk. 'It's sort of my fault too,' I said at last. 'You've not been happy and I suppose I didn't get in your shoes. Gran told me that's what you should do but maybe nobody's very good at imagining what other people think. You sort of believe you're the main person and everything and everybody is less important.'

He grinned. 'Like that poor old Fay. I suppose she was weird because her father beat her up. Dad says we're going to have her round sometimes. I guess I'll get used to her.'

I didn't think he knew the full story about Gran's death and Fay's part in it or he would have said something about it. I was just going to tell him myself when I changed my mind. After all, Fay would still be living next door. I felt almost as if my dear gran was in the room now telling me that the fewer people who knew what Fay had done the better.

Matthew came back. 'It was rather horrible.' He frowned. 'I found bits of dolls – china heads – legs and arms. Almost as if real people had been burned! Izzy said that Mrs G. told her it was a big collection of dolls and quite valuable.' He noticed my new camera on the dresser. 'Taken any pictures yet, Fran? I'm sorry but the village shop only had a film with twelve negs. on it.'

113

I remembered the picture of Denny. I wanted to show it to her. 'There's just two more on it. If we took those, could you take the film to be developed in the town – one of those quick places?'

'All right. Impatient like your mum, aren't you?' He picked up the camera and took a picture of me and Jez, then Obediah looking down at the dogs from his perch on the windowsill. 'By the way, Fay came round early with the forty pounds. Could you pay the furniture man this time, Fran?' He was smiling as he went out with Jez.

It seemed impossible that I would be going back to school with Jez, in a week's time. I felt as if I had been to a different country – the strange land of death.

The furniture man came with the bookcase. 'All there today,' he said, winking as I gave him the money.

I was looking at the remains of the barn, which were just as grisly as Matthew had said, when I heard the dogs barking and found them both back from the town. 'Here you are, and thanks.' Slightly pink-faced, Jez shoved a box of chocolates into my hands. He went off, muttering about putting the wheel on his bike again.

'Did the one-hour development,' Matthew said, handing me the photos.

He looked over my shoulder as I flipped through them. 'That's an interesting one,' he said.

Bas and Sophie were looking up at a shaft of sunshine coming through the trees. There was no sign of Denny.

'Clever of you to get them to look up – it's almost as if there was someone there,' he went on while I held the

114

negatives up to the light. They must have made a mistake in the printing. No, here it was – the two dogs – and nobody else. Where was Denny?

Later, we picnicked under the apple tree. It was hot again and very still. Gran used to say in September that the garden was holding its breath, ready for winter. I'd calmed down a bit about the photograph and tried to convince myself that I'd got my thumb over the lens or something. I remembered Denny saying, 'Hope the photo comes out.' I had to see her and thank her for helping rescue Jez.

Matthew was drinking from a can of beer. 'Just like a holiday,' he said.

'We ought to get a hammock,' Jez said sleepily and in a minute, he was out like a light.

'Tired, after last night,' his dad said. 'And what about you, Fran?'

'My arms and legs are a bit stiff from the swimming.'

'I'll drive you over to Mrs Hardy this afternoon. I expect she'll bring you back.'

Two red apples fell in my lap. I looked up and saw the branches shaking although there wasn't a breath of wind.

We left Jez asleep. 'Best not to tell anyone what Fay did to the boat, nor about her candles,' Matthew said in the car and I agreed.

Matthew told Hills all about the fire and about my getting Jez out of the river and rescuing Fay from the fire. I was just going to tell her that Denny had helped me when Matthew said he had to go. Hills offered to bring me back and in the end, I never told her.

'Your gran would have been very proud of you.' Hills gave me a big hug. 'Tea first, then photographs. Did you find out any more about her death?'

I followed her into the kitchen while she boiled the kettle. 'I've found out from the Goodings it was just a terrible accident. Robin got in the boat and it somehow floated off. Gran rescued him but the shock and the cold water was too much for her heart.'

'So it was an accident, as we'd thought.' She filled the teapot, then blew her nose loudly on a piece of kitchen towel. 'Just like Frances, daft thing trying to swim in a nightdress in that cold water! I'm proud of her but oh dear, how I miss her!'

While we had tea, she talked brightly of the time she and Gran were at school in Denesford in the war – of helping with the harvest, of riding cart-horses, of evacuees and unexploded bombs and flying bombs she called doodlebugs. 'She was always the leader – and we got into trouble quite a bit!' She laughed. 'We were what they called tomboys – always climbing trees, sliding down straw-stacks, riding ponies bareback in the field – and falling off! I was the evacuee from London, staying at Folly Farm, you know. I loved the village so much I spent the rest of my life here.'

She fetched her ancient album, filled with those mini black and white snaps they had in the olden days. She flipped through some of herself – there was a village school picture but I could hardly see Gran, it was so small. She turned a page and a piece of paper fell out. I noticed it was in my gran's writing.

'That's a poem your gran liked and wrote out for me not long ago. She knew I collected bits of poetry,' Hills said. 'I showed it to your mother when she came to arrange the funeral. She wrote down the first two lines and had them carved on the gravestone. Do you want to keep it?'

I put it in my jeans pocket to read later.

Hills was turning the pages of the album. 'Look at this one! I took it with my first camera – I brought it out to the hayfield. I remember, Denny said she was all mucky and didn't want me to take it.'

Denny – what did she mean? I stared at the photo. This one was sharper. It *was* Denny – laughing on top of a load of hay! She was wearing shorts and wellies, and her plaits were coming undone. I kept staring, unable to believe what I saw.

Hills was still talking. 'We all called your gran Denny in those days – as you probably know, her surname before she married Sam Lee was Denton. She dressed like a boy – didn't care what she looked like – but she was pretty, really. I was so pleased when she came back to settle at Folly Farm after Sam died. You know, she loved you a lot, Fran. I expect you feel her presence still in the house, in a way.'

Or down by the river. I stared, not really able to take it in. My thoughts whirled round in my head. Had I been meeting a ghost – the ghost of Gran as a child? Or was it more like a time-slip? She had seemed so solid, so real. I didn't know whether I wanted to cry or laugh – or was I scared? It just seemed awesome and incredible.

'Are you all right?' Hills asked. 'You've gone so pale. I'm sorry – I suppose seeing these photos of your gran brought it all back.'

'Fine,' I muttered – but I felt mega-weird – almost as if I were in some kind of dream. That moment was printed on my brain for all time: the grandfather clock's deliberate tick-tock, the taste of chocolate cake and the sharp smell of huge russet chrysanths, massed in a vase in the hearth.

I realised Hills was still talking: '...and your gran told me she hoped she'd always be around to help you, until you grew up.' She closed the album with a sigh.

On the way home, in Hills' car, I was silent, thinking of all the clues I'd had about Denny: the remarks she'd made, the knowledge she'd had about the Goodings. The gap in my photograph...I supposed some of the time she had been invisible – like when she threw apples down from the tree. I thought Sophie had seen her, many times. Where did Denny go when she left me? Did she know she was a ghost? Would she come back again? Oh, how I wanted to see her, ghost or not.

I had to find her. I waited that evening until Mum was busy with her paperwork for Jeans Unlimited and Matthew and Jez were playing a computer game.

*

I go into the cool, autumn-smelling woods. The sun is setting. The dogs walk sedately beside me, down the track to the river and through the bushes to the den.

The water is glowing pink-gold in the sunset. I tell the dogs to sit. I climb along the willow-trunk and dangle my feet above the placid river. Already the water has gone down and the banks no longer overflow. There's a noise... but it's squirrels, chasing through the trees, arguing with each other. Two moorhens chunter towards me, then take fright and fly off. A fish rises and plops at a fly.

Suddenly I know, almost as if I can hear her speak, that I am not going to see Denny again. She'd come back to help me and now she's gone... where? 'You have to let your gran go,' she'd said in the churchyard.

There's a flash of blue, darting between the banks, disappearing upstream. I shall bring Jez and Fay here, to see the kingfisher. I know when I come back, talking to Denny will seem like a dream... already the reality is fading fast. I remember the paper in my pocket and take it out. My gran's writing is like her, curved, generous, bold.

Do not stand by my grave and weep.
I am not there. I do not sleep.
I am a thousand winds that blow.
I am the diamond glint in snow.
I am the sunlight on ripe grain.
I am the gentle autumn rain.
Awakening in the morning's hush

I am the swift uplifting rush
Of quiet birds in circling flight.
I am the star that shines at night.
Do not stand at my grave and cry.
I am not there. I did not die.

The dogs are whining. Sophie looks past me to the opposite bank and slowly wags her tail. Bas copies her. What can they see?

I wave, just in case.